Camden Town Tales

Stuck
On
Me

Hilary Freeman

Piccadilly Press • London

To my gorgeous cousin,
Anna Corre

First published in Great Britain in 2012
by Piccadilly Press Ltd,
5 Castle Road, London NW1 8PR
www.piccadillypress.co.uk

A catalogue record for this book is available
from the British Library

ISBN: 978 1 84812 131 7 (paperback)
ISBN: 978 1 84812 203 1 (ebook)

1 3 5 7 9 10 8 6 4 2

Printed and bound by CPI Group (UK) Ltd,
Croydon, CR0 4YY
Cover design by Simon Davis
Cover illustrations by Susan Hellard

Hi!

Camden Town is one of the most colourful places in the world, with a unique mix of styles and cultures. Come here and you'll see emos and cyberpunks, rockabillies, mods and indie kids . . . the list goes on and on. It truly is a place where you can dress outlandishly, and nobody blinks an eye.

But when you're a teenager, even in Camden, it can be difficult to accept the way you look, especially if you don't have conventionally 'beautiful' features or a model figure. When I was younger I hated my big nose and frizzy hair and longed for straight, glossy locks and petite features, like the girls I considered to be pretty (and the ones I thought the boys liked). It took me many years – and lots of experiments with hair products – to learn how to make the best of my looks and, finally, to accept myself.

In *Stuck on Me*, Sky faces similar thoughts, but is helped by her best friends Rosie and Vix. I hope that you'll enjoy the ride and, if you're not entirely happy with the way you look, that reading this book will also help you to like yourself a little more too.

Love,

Hilary

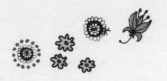

Prologue

We're at the Dublin Castle on Camden Parkway, a venue where every band you've ever heard of – and loads you haven't – has played. It's absolutely heaving. You can hardly hear the music over the chatter and the clinking of beer glasses. Nobody has asked our ages yet. If we keep our heads down, don't try to buy drinks and blend into the crowd, nobody will take any notice of us. People always say that I look older than fourteen; Rosie too. Even Vix can get away with it when she dresses up and puts on eyeliner, like tonight. We're not planning to stay too long, anyway. Just a quick look around, to see if he's there, and then out again. If he is . . . well, I haven't even imagined what will happen then.

1

We push past the bar towards the back, where the bands perform. There's a group of old-timers on stage, guys in their fifties who look like they've been gigging for years. They're playing some vintage blues music, which I recognise from Mum's CDs. I quite like it, although I'd never admit that to her.

I take Rosie's and Vix's arms and steer them through the crowd, so that we can get a better view of the stage. I look from left to right, checking each musician off my list: pony-tailed singer and guitarist – not him; black bassist – not him; bald, lanky drummer – not him.

Then I see the harmonica player and my knees buckle.

'Oh my God. Oh my God,' I whisper, aware that nobody can hear me. I feel sick, my legs are like jelly. I cling on to my friends' arms for support.

Vix grasps my hand and squeezes my fingers tight. 'What, Sky?' she asks, concerned. 'What is it? Are you OK?'

I realise I'm shaking. 'The guy with the harmonica,' I shout into her ear, my voice thin and squeaky. 'Look. Over there.'

He's standing to the side of the stage, wearing baggy, faded jeans and a shirt that could do with ironing, the buttons straining at his belly. His hair is thinner than I remember but still dark and wavy, although there are traces of grey in his chin stubble. He looks tired, ill and bloated, and it makes me feel sad, even though I swore I'd never care about him again.

'Are you sure?' mouths Rosie.

'It's him,' I stutter. 'We've found him. Look at his profile, when he turns. It's exactly the same as mine, isn't it?'

'Really? Wow!' Rosie starts to walk forward to get a better view, *but I drag her back, into the darkness. I don't want him to notice me. Not yet.*

I have no doubt that it's him. Looking at his face is like looking at an older, more weathered, male version of me.

I guess it's true what they say. If you want to find something – or someone – all you have to do is follow your nose . . .

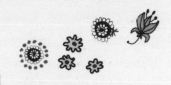

Chapter 1

The Pinocchio Complex

'So, do you like my new dress?' asks Rosie, striding and twirling around her bedroom as if she's on the catwalk at London Fashion Week, while Vix and I gaze up at her from her bed. 'Very retro-chic, don't you think?'

'Love it,' says Vix, without hesitation.

I stare at Rosie, trying to find something positive to say about her latest Stables Market find. The dress is ancient (from the seventies), smells like mothballs and has a horrible orange flower pattern on it. It doesn't even fit her properly. There's only one word for it: rank.

'Um . . .' I begin. I want to lie, I really do. I don't want to hurt Rosie's feelings. 'Um . . .'

Lying would be the kind thing to do, wouldn't it? Rosie doesn't want to know what I think; she just wants admiration. But, unfortunately, I just have to tell the truth. 'Um, sorry, but I don't really like it,' I say, finally. 'If I'm honest, it's a bit big for you. And it looks like it needs a good wash. You've got much nicer dresses.'

Vix's mouth falls open in shock. 'Sky, what's got into you?'

Rosie looks at me, hurt. 'Blunt much?' She glances down at her dress, grimaces and starts to remove it. She'll probably never wear it out now. I feel bad.

'I'm sorry, Rosie,' I say. 'I'm not being nasty. But I really *can't* lie to you.'

I can lie, obviously – I'm quite capable of it and I've done it in the past, usually just to be kind – but, as of today, I've decided that from now on, I mustn't. I'm far too superstitious and it's much too risky. Why? Because if I ever do lie again, there's the tiniest chance that the story Mum read to me as a child will come true. My nose might start growing, Pinocchio-stylee. And that, frankly, would be a disaster on a world-ending scale.

I'm not exaggerating. My nose already casts its own shadow. A few more centimetres and it could block out the sun.

'Don't be stupid, you don't have a big nose,' says Rosie, when I explain this to her, by way of an apology for being rude about her dress. 'It's a normal-sized nose.'

I roll my eyes. 'Normal-sized for an anteater, maybe.'

'Oh Sky, don't be so down on yourself,' says Vix. 'I never even noticed your nose until you pointed it out. I always notice your pretty eyes, or your hair. There's nothing wrong with your nose.'

They're both lying, of course. Lying to make me feel better. But it's easy for them; they don't have to worry about the consequences. Vix has a tiny, doll-sized nose and Rosie has a perfectly proportioned, sharp little nose that fits the rest of her features. Mine looks like it's been stuck on me like Mr Potato Head's. I really must have told a hell of a lot of lies in a previous life to deserve my hooter. Or maybe I *was* an anteater in a previous life.

'Absolute nonsense,' said Mum, when I once suggested this explanation. 'You were definitely an Egyptian princess. I can see it in your aura.'

My mum believes in all that stuff: reincarnation, karma, chanting mantras and recycling compost. That's why she took me and my sisters on a retreat in Goa recently. And why she persuaded me to have my nose pierced while we were there. Most mums would have tried to talk their fourteen-year-old daughter out of it. Not my mum. She encouraged it, and then she had hers done too. And now we've both got little red, sparkly jewels to the side of our right nostrils. Big mistake. My nose stud is like a neon sign, proclaiming: Big Nose Right Here.

Rosie and Vix disagree, of course. They think my nose stud looks cool.

'I wish I could get one done, but Mum would kill me,' says Rosie, stroking her neat little nostril. 'She'd go on about hygiene and hepatitis and sharing needles. I'm not even allowed to get my ears pierced until I'm sixteen.'

'You don't know how lucky you are,' I say. 'Mum had my ears pierced when I was a baby. I didn't get a choice. My baby photos look like an advert for Claire's Accessories.'

'If you hate it that much, take it out,' says Vix, always practical. 'You'll probably have to for school, anyway. But I think it suits you.'

'I tried that,' I tell her, 'but it just leaves a slightly scabby hole, which looks even worse.'

'It'll heal over. And in the meantime, there's always concealer.'

'Hmm. That's true. I wonder if I can conceal my whole nose?'

Vix slaps me playfully on the arm. 'There is nothing wrong with your nose. Believe me. You're gorgeous.'

'Yeah, and you need glasses.'

I wish I *could* believe Vix and Rosie. But the evidence that they're wrong is everywhere I look: in reflections, in photographs, in the shadows on my bedroom wall at night that make me look so witch-like in silhouette that I frighten myself. Every morning, when I stare in the mirror, my nose appears to have grown longer and beakier, as if it's making a bid for freedom from my face. I know I've been going through what Mum calls a growth spurt, with my arms and legs and torso lengthening and even the shape of my face becoming leaner and less squishy. But my nose? It's sprinting ahead of the rest of my features. The scariest thing is, I don't know where the finish line is.

My nose even gets in the way when I kiss my boyfriend, Rich. I can't remember it being a problem in the past but now, every time we go in for a snog, our noses bash into each other, and we end up doing this stupid dance with our heads until we find a better position, by which time we don't feel much like kissing any more. Rich doesn't have a big nose, so it must be my fault.

'When did your nose start bothering you so much?' asks Rosie, coming to sit beside me on the bed. She's taken off the vile orange dress and put her jeans and T-shirt back on. 'You never used to have a problem with it.'

'When it started growing out of proportion to the rest of my face,' I say. 'I'm surprised I haven't felt growing pains.'

Rosie laughs. 'What *are* you on about, Sky? You look the same as you always have. Just not like a little kid any more.'

'Yeah, your face has got character,' says Vix.

'Thanks.' I bristle. She means it as a compliment, but I know what 'character' means: it's another word for ugly. Girls with *characterful* faces never get to play the love interest in movies; they're always the sisters or best friends.

I want to change the subject now. Rosie and Vix are both staring at my face so intently that I'm beginning to feel uncomfortable.

'Forget it,' I say. 'It's not important. Let's watch a DVD or something.'

'Sure thing,' says Rosie. 'Just don't worry about it, OK?'

'Course not,' I promise, discreetly crossing my fingers. 'I won't mention it ever again.'

But as I say this, I'm sure I can feel a little tickle in the tip of my nose, as it extends by yet another millimetre.

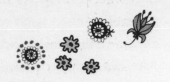

Chapter 2
Thirty Metres Off The Ground

Rich and I have been together for ages, longer than any other couple I know. We're coming up to our six-month anniversary. That's serious. '*Too* serious,' Mum says. She thinks I should be 'playing the field' but what does she know? She hasn't had a proper boyfriend since Dad left. I'm pretty sure I love Rich and he told me he loves me too, although he hasn't said it for a while (if I think about it). And (if I think about it harder), he's never said it first. I'd rather not think about that, though, because it makes me miserable. It's bad enough that I've hardly seen him this summer, although that's not really his fault – I was in Goa for weeks and we couldn't talk or message each other very often. If my mum weren't so dippy, I might wonder if she planned the holiday just to split us up.

I really missed Rich while I was away. I thought about him all the time and I didn't even check out anybody else. Although, to be fair, I didn't meet many guys who didn't have long, white beards. And long, curly toenails. Rich says he missed me too but . . . I don't know. Something seems different now. I've been back for nearly a fortnight and we've only met up alone twice, for a couple of hours, and once it was just so I could help him buy some new trainers. At the beginning, he'd come round all the time, to talk and listen to music and stuff in my bedroom, but lately he seems to want us to go out with his mates instead.

Just like today. I've rung Rich because we have a vague arrangement to spend the day together, doing something fun, before school starts tomorrow. And, if I'm honest, I'd also like to ask him if everything is all right between us. And if he thinks that my nose has grown since I went to Goa. And if that's why he seems to be avoiding me.

'Hey, Rich,' I say, when he finally picks up. 'Are you coming round, then?'

'I can't,' he says, without even seeming to think about it. 'I'm with my mates.'

'Oh, right. It's just that I thought you said we'd see each other today. I'd like to see you. I want to talk . . .'

I shouldn't have said that. I swear I can hear him bristle. 'What about?'

'Um . . .' What I really want to say is 'About *us*' but I know that will sound serious and make him freak out. And I can't say, 'About my nose' either, because that sounds ridiculous. 'Nothing special. Just stuff.'

'What stuff?' His voice becomes a whisper, as if he doesn't want his mates to hear. 'You're not going all weird on me, are you?'

'No, of course not.'

'Right, well, I was going to text you anyway,' he says, louder again. 'I thought we could all go out together. To the bank holiday fair.'

'Oh. I guess. I kind of thought we could have a day for just the two of us.'

'Yeah, but we can do that any time. Why don't you ask Rosie and Vix if they want to come too?'

'OK, sure,' I say, even though I haven't planned to see my friends today. I told them I'd be seeing Rich for a romantic afternoon, and if I tell them it's turned into a group thing now they'll start nagging me again about how Rich isn't treating me right. Still, it's better than staying in on my own. I know Rosie is meeting her brand new boyfriend Laurie, but she can drag him along if she wants. Vix doesn't like Rich's mates, although she'll be sweet and friendly to their faces. If I'm honest, I don't much like them either. They're loud and lairy, and they make Rich act the same way.

'Cool. See you at Camden Road at three, then?'

'Yeah,' I say. I take a deep breath. 'Love you.'

But he's already gone.

A few hours later, I'm standing outside Camden Road railway station with Vix, waiting for Rich to show up. Rosie has decided not to come; she said she wants to get to know Laurie better first before she brings him out in public. I'm starting to think that I should have just told Rich that I'd see him tonight instead. There's a fair at Hampstead Heath every bank holiday and I always seem to end up going along with friends, even though I never enjoy myself much. I don't like the crowds, or the rides which make me feel dizzy and sick and mess up my hair. The only thing I do like are the dodgems. And the candy floss. I've never told anyone that before; you're supposed to love fairs, aren't you, especially if you're a teen? That's why they're called 'fun' fairs. Yeah, sure. About as fun as doing your maths homework, but hanging upside down by your legs, thirty metres off the ground.

'Hey,' says Rich, rolling up with three of his most annoying mates in tow. I only know one of them: Luke, a guy from school, who still looks like he's about eight and acts like it too. Rich gives me a peck on the cheek, which is almost, but not quite, as passionate as the one I gave my mum when I left the flat. However, it still inspires Luke to make loud squelching noises and to rub his hands up and down his chest like he's having the steamiest snog ever.

Vix rolls her eyes at me. I know she's thinking, What on earth do you want a boyfriend for?

'Let's go,' I say, embarrassed. I grasp Vix's arm and we walk ahead of the boys, through the ticket barrier and up the stairs to the platform. We can hear them behind us, jostling each other and throwing bits of paper at our backs. Rich is never like this when he's on his own with me. It's weird: the moment his mates show up he starts behaving like he's a monkey in a cage at London Zoo.

Hampstead Heath isn't far from Camden, just a few stops on the Overground line, but it's a world apart. It's much more chichi than Camden – full of delis and duck ponds and posh people. It's also incredibly green, like the countryside, which you wouldn't expect to find in London. There's acres of woodland, with every tree, flower, bird and butterfly you can imagine. Mum used to take us here for walks and nature trails when we were little. She picked mushrooms here too, until she accidentally poisoned us all with a stir-fry and decided she'd be wiser to buy them from the Wholefoods shop on Parkway instead.

The walk from the station to the fair, which has been set up at the start of the Heath, only takes a few minutes. As we draw closer, we can hear an eerie mix of sounds – strains of music, laughter and distant screams. The pavement is littered with hotdog cartons and empty Coke cans, which Rich and his mates kick back and forth like footballs. Rich still hasn't said more than two words to me; it's like I'm invisible.

'Do I look all right?' I whisper to Vix. I've made a big effort with my make-up today and I'm wearing my most flattering skinny jeans.

'You look great!' she says. 'Gorgeous.'

'Thanks.' I force a smile. I don't feel much better, though, because she's not the person I want to hear it from.

The fair is coming into view now, appearing like a field of giant, brightly coloured skeletons against the trees. We enter and walk around for a while, viewing the rides with their flashing lights, the shooting games that no one ever wins, and the stalls selling sweets and food.

'So what are we going on first?' asks Rich. 'Shall we start big? Or build up to it?'

'What about that one?' says one of his mates, pointing up at the sky.

'Yeah, good one!' says Rich. 'I'm game.'

We've stopped beside the scariest, meanest-looking ride in the whole fair. It's called the Looping Screamer and it's one of those rollercoasters that not only goes incredibly high and incredibly fast, but also corkscrews around, propelling you upside down. I look up at it and my knees buckle. 'Um . . . I'm not sure I want to go on that,' I say, hanging back.

Rich walks over to me. For a moment I think he's going to give me a hug, but he doesn't. 'Don't be a wuss, Sky,' he says, impatiently.

'I'm not . . . I just don't really like rides that make you go upside down like that. Can't we go on the dodgems instead?'

'Nah, we'll do that later. Come on, it'll be fun. Everyone's waiting.'

He's right – the others have joined the queue already.

Rich's mates are full of bravado; Luke is making clucking noises at me.

'Can't I wait for you here? I'll get us some drinks.'

'Don't be such a killjoy!'

'OK,' I say reluctantly, giving in. I wish I could be stronger, but I want to please Rich and I don't want everyone to think I'm a scaredy cat; they'll tease me for the rest of the day.

'Right, so you'll ride with Vix, then,' says Rich.

'Oh . . .' I want to say, 'I'd rather sit with you so I can hold your hand,' but that makes me sound even more of a wuss. 'OK, then.'

I walk over to Vix and take her arm again.

'You all right?' she asks.

I nod.

When we reach the front of the queue, the ride moves around to meet us. We climb into our seats and the bar automatically comes down over our laps, trapping us. It's too late to change my mind now. I turn to face Vix. 'I might grab your hand,' I warn.

She smiles at me, reassuringly. 'Fine, as long as you don't throw up on me!'

Vix loves rides: the higher and faster the better. She's a real speed demon. You'd never think it to look at her. She seems so calm and quiet and sensible.

There's a mechanical groaning noise and the ride begins to move. It's deceptively slow at first, and I think, maybe, I can handle this. But then we start to pick up speed and my fear takes over. The people around me begin to scream, like they're being massacred in the most horrific way. I don't scream. I just screw up my eyes and clench my teeth and cling onto the bar in front of me praying that it won't spring open and fling me across the Heath to my death. The ride seems to go on for ever, lurching this way and that, throwing me sideways against the metal of my seat and bruising my thighs. I can feel the wind whipping against my face, and my hair blowing out in all directions. My stomach feels like it's in motion, rolling around my insides and trying to find an exit. This is truly horrible. I want it to stop. Please make it stop! I want to get off!

Hours and hours seem to pass and then we're slowing down again. There's a juddering noise and, my eyes still closed, I realise we've come to a standstill. The bar lifts from my lap and, gingerly, I open my eyes. The world is still spinning. When I try to climb out of my seat, I lose my balance and have to sit back down again.

'That was cool, wasn't it?!' says Vix, helping me out. Her cheeks are flushed and she's grinning, like she's had the best time ever.

'It was OK,' I manage to say. 'Could have been worse. I'm glad it's over.' I glance around for Rich. He's standing by the entrance, looking rather pale. Luke is being sick. The others are laughing at him. I laugh too, on the inside.

'So what's next?' asks Rich.

'Dodgems!' I shout, before anyone else can suggest another ride that's not firmly rooted to the ground. I've noticed that another of Rich's mates has been evilly eyeing up the Twister.

'Cool,' says Vix. 'Let's get a car each.'

'Fine by me.' I'm planning to ram Rich's car really hard to punish him for making me get on that rollercoaster.

I do a pretty good job, although I almost give myself whiplash in the process. In fact, I have so much fun that I insist we have another go. I think I like the dodgems so much because we don't have a car at home. You don't really need one in Camden – the public transport's so good, and you can walk through Regent's Park into the centre of London in half an hour. But Mum wouldn't drive, even if we lived in the countryside. She'd probably make us travel by horse and cart. She says cars are evil polluters, which are destroying the environment. I can't wait until I'm seventeen and can learn to drive myself.

The next couple of hours are, surprisingly, quite enjoyable. I manage to avoid going on any more of the really scary rides by volunteering to fetch drinks and hotdogs for everyone and slipping off to find a toilet at opportune moments. One of Rich's mates, a guy called Robbie, takes a shine to Vix and keeps trying to sit next to her. She's not interested at all. I can't blame her – he's got bum fluff and, ironically, no bum (which is very clear because his trousers keep slipping halfway down his thighs). Every time I walk behind him, all I can think about is hitching them up for him. I'm so lucky to have Rich: he's cute and stylish and funny. I just know that if I get to spend any proper time alone with him, things will go back to the way they were before I went to Goa.

Chapter 3

The Wicked Witch
Of The West

It's after six and almost time to go home. We've all had too many hotdogs and too many sweets and we're tired, but nobody wants to leave yet. Even me. School starts tomorrow and we all know that when we arrive home the summer holidays will be over.

'Let's go on one more ride before we leave,' says Rich. He puts his hand in his pocket and pulls out the last of his loose change. 'Bummer. No cash left. What can we do for one pound fifty?'

'Good question,' says Vix, shutting her purse with a click. 'This place has cleaned me out. I've got about the same.'

The other boys have virtually nothing left either, and I only have a couple of quid. So we wander around again for a while. Most of the rides, except the kiddie ones, cost at least two pounds a go. Nobody but me fancies the carousel (too old school) or the helter skelter (too boring). We were planning a trip on the ghost train, but that costs three quid.

'How about the house of mirrors?' I suggest. The others aren't impressed. Vix decides she'd rather have a can of Coke. Spotting an opportunity to be alone with Rich, I try to persuade him to join me. 'Oh go on, Rich. Come with me. It's no fun alone.'

'Yeah,' says Luke. 'Go with her. It will be dark in there, won't it?' He winks at Rich.

'Why not?' says Rich. He turns to the others. 'Wait for us here, OK?'

We wander up a plank into the 'house', which is really a shed on stilts, decorated with pictures of contorted faces. It's dimly lit inside, and slightly spooky, so I take Rich's hand. The mirrors are arranged in a maze of rooms, lighting up and appearing unexpectedly from the darkness as we pass by. The first mirror makes me look ten feet tall and as skinny as a supermodel. I like this mirror. I wish I could take it home with me and put it in my bag to bring out in shop changing rooms. The second has the opposite effect, making me look squat and round. Rich giggles. He puts his hand around my waist and squeezes it, affectionately.

'You can talk,' I say, as he comes into view in the same

mirror. 'Who's been eating too many pies, then?'

Rich laughs again, then turns me around and draws me close to him. He puts his hand on the back of my neck and strokes my hair. We find ourselves kissing, slowly, gently. I feel happy, for the first time in weeks.

'We look like two teletubbies snogging,' I say. Rich laughs again and pinches my cheek. I pluck up my courage and say, 'I've missed you.'

'Yeah,' he says. 'I know. Yeah, me too. Come on . . .' He takes my hand and we walk deeper into the maze, laughing at our images in a wavy mirror and in another that makes us look as small as ants. In the next room there are several mirrors and we are reflected multiple times, as if the whole world is populated only by versions of me and Rich. I think about his mates outside, and wish that could be true. We kiss again and, for a few moments, it is.

Then we turn a corner and find ourselves in the centre of the maze, in a room in which every mirror presents a more distorted reflection than the last. One makes me look as if I don't have a head at all, just a pinprick on my shoulders. Another chops me off at the waist, so I'm like a torso, with arms, floating in the air. But it's the third that makes me stop in my tracks, my stomach lurching faster and harder than it did on the rollercoaster . . . because the image it shows does not seem that distorted at all: it's the way I see myself every time I look at my reflection. Before me, I can see a monster, with a huge hooked nose, tiny eyes and a tiny mouth. The face is grotesque. The face is mine.

I stand, rooted to the spot, unable to stop looking. I'm the Wicked Witch of the West. All I need is a broomstick.

'Come on,' says Rich. 'We've been in here ages. The others are waiting.'

'Hold on, Rich. Can I ask you something? Do I really look like that?'

'Don't be stupid.'

'I know, but look at my nose! It's deformed.'

He laughs. 'Yeah, so is mine. Look at my nose in there. I look like a freak. That's what the mirror's meant to do.'

I can see that his nose is distorted in the mirror, larger and longer than it really is. He looks weird. But I don't, not really. My nose looks the way it always does, just slightly more exaggerated.

'Bend down,' he says. I obey. 'See, now you've got a weird forehead instead.'

'Yeah, but my nose still looks huge.'

'No it doesn't.'

'Honest? Even in real life? You don't think it's grown?'

'Jesus, Sky. What's up with you?' He takes my hand again but, this time, he drags me by it, hard. 'Let's go back and look in the fat mirror again instead. That made you laugh.'

'No, I don't want to.' I'm aware I'm feeling tearful and that my voice sounds whiny, but I can't help myself. 'Seriously, you don't think I have a ginormous nose? Be honest with me, please.'

Rich rolls his eyes. 'God, Sky, shut up about your stupid nose.' He drops my hand and begins walking towards the exit, alone. 'I don't know what's up with you lately. I tell you what, though – you're seriously no fun any more.'

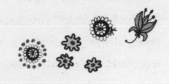

Chapter 4

Connor Carter's Conk

If I think about it, I can pinpoint the exact moment when I started obsessing about my nose. I'd noticed it had changed before, of course, but it didn't start to keep me awake at night until the day my aunties came round for tea, just before I went to Goa . . .

'Goodness, Sky, haven't you grown!' declared Auntie Karen, kissing me loudly on both cheeks. I cringed, like I always do. She's being saying this to me and to my sisters, Grass and Ocean, at every family get-together since I can remember. I think someone must pay her to embarrass us; she certainly acts like it's her job.

She took a step back. 'You do look ever so grown up.'

'Thanks, Auntie Karen.' I forced a smile and, when I was sure she wasn't looking, wiped her wet, peach lipstick imprint from my cheek. Dealing with embarrassing aunties was *so* not the way I wanted to be spending the last Sunday afternoon before I went away for a month.

'No, I really mean it, dear. Let me look at you.' She took my face in her hands and squeezed my cheeks, as if they were made out of playdough. 'You're different,' she continued. 'Still lovely, of course, but your face . . . it's more defined. No more puppy fat, eh? Those boys will be queuing up.' She prodded the side of my nose. Her hands smelled of onions. 'And you certainly don't have a little baby nose any more, eh?'

I did a double take. Did she really just say that aloud? Did Auntie Karen really just tell me – and everyone else – that I have a big nose? Grass giggled; I must have heard right. Aware that I was glowing bright red, I stepped away from Auntie Karen and went to sit down on the sofa, covering my nose with my palm, protectively.

So it isn't just me, then, I thought, mortified. My nose is huge and people can tell!

'You're right, Karen,' said Auntie Julie. 'Sky looks terribly grown up.' She stared at me too – although, thankfully, she didn't feel the need to touch my face. Then she appeared to have a lightbulb moment. 'I know! I've got it! Doesn't she look like Connor all of a sudden?'

It took me a second to twig exactly who Connor was. I've

never called him that. I felt a twinge of nausea rise from my belly.

'I didn't . . . you know, you might be right,' said Mum, in a weird voice, peering at me, as if she had never seen me before. I was starting to feel like an exhibit in a science lab. 'I hadn't really noticed the change,' she continued. 'I guess you don't see someone growing when you're with them every day. But Julie's spot on. You've gone and got your dad's nose, Sky. Well, well, well.'

I looked around the table from my mother to my older sister, Ocean, and then to my younger sister, Grass. It struck me that all three of them have exactly the same slender nose, with slightly triangular nostrils and a cute little tip. Perfectly proportioned identikit noses, which looked like they'd been made to a pattern in the same factory. Grass could be my mum's Mini-me, they're so similar. Mum often likes to pretend we're all sisters. She gets a buzz when people say, 'Oh but you don't look old enough to be a mother yet, let alone have three such grown-up teenage daughters!'

I hadn't acknowledged it before, but that day it became clear to me that I don't really look like her, or the others. I've got her eyes, maybe, but I'm taller, darker, flatter chested. And if my nose was made in the same factory, it was in the mis-shape pile, rejected for being too big and slightly wonky.

Until that second I had never wanted to look like Mum. In fact, I've tried my hardest not to, refusing to wear the hippy-dippy clothes she likes me to dress in, and cutting my hair to shoulder length, when she'd prefer me to wear it down to my waist. But now I felt like the odd one out. And I didn't like it.

'You've got no reason to feel self-conscious, Sky. It's a handsome nose,' said Mum.

'Gee, thanks, just what I've always wanted – a handsome nose,' I said, hoping sarcasm would mask my hurt.

Mum smiled, wistfully. 'Oh, but Connor had a lovely nose. A real Roman nose. It was one of the things I first noticed about him. That, and his eyes.'

'Yes, he was a nice-looking fellow,' said Auntie Julie. 'That's one thing we can all say.'

I flinched. They were talking about him like he was dead. But he isn't dead. He's just . . . somewhere else. He left when I was eight and then there were a couple of years of odd weekend visits and random cards. After that, nothing. I haven't heard from him for almost five years. We used to get bits of news through Grandma, but since she died: nada.

'Oh, sure, he was a handsome devil,' said Auntie Karen, winking at Mum. 'Devil being the operative word.'

Mum nodded. Then she shook her head, as if she was trying to shake off her memories. 'Well, it's all in the past now. No point dwelling on it.'

She tried to change the subject then, as usual; she doesn't like talking about Dad. Since he left, Mum has filled the gap – and our flat – with all her weird and wonderful interests, and the new friends that come with them: animal rights, spirituality, medieval music, saving the planet . . . She claims she's a free spirit. Who needs a man, when you can do a thousand and one things with tofu?

But I didn't want to drop the subject. 'He wasn't a devil, he was my dad,' I said, quietly. 'He's *still* my dad. *Our* dad.' Even if, I wanted to add, he doesn't care about me, Ocean or Grass enough to remember our birthdays, or send us Christmas presents. I glanced at my sisters, but they were staring down at their plates, pretending they weren't there.

'Of course he is,' said Mum, 'but we're OK without him, aren't we? Us girls together!'

I nodded. 'Sure. I guess.' As always, I felt strange thinking about Dad. I hate him and I love him and I miss him and I don't miss him, all at the same time. It's so confusing.

Mum peered at me again, and I couldn't tell if she was calculating how much I resembled Dad or whether she was just concerned about me. 'I know you miss him sometimes, Sky. But you're better off without him. We all are.'

'Yeah. Probably.' I grinned broadly, a fake grin. 'But I shouldn't moan – at least he gave me something,' I joked, 'even if it was his great, big, beaky nose. Cheers, Dad.'

Nobody laughed.

'Another slice of cake, girls?' said Auntie Julie, to break the tension. 'This spelt cake really is good.'

I managed to get through the rest of the tea somehow, making small talk with my aunties about how I was doing at school and what GCSEs I'd chosen, but I couldn't stop thinking about my dad, and how unfair it was that I was the one to look like him, when he made all of us so unhappy. The minute my aunties left the flat, I went into my bedroom, shut the door tight and fished around under my bed until I found my old photo albums. Then I leafed through them, hunting for pictures of my dad. I don't have many, I realised with sadness: just a few old snaps of him holding me as a baby, and some from one Christmas when I was six or seven. And there were also a couple of photographs of him with Mum when they first met, pictures she was planning to throw out when she was really upset once, and that I rescued. She doesn't know I have them.

I studied the photos, taking each one out and holding it up to my face in the mirror, so that I could compare my features with Dad's. There was no getting away from it: Mum was right – I do have Dad's nose. His is almost exactly the same shape as mine – slightly more crooked, perhaps (I think I remember him telling me that he broke it in an accident, when he was a kid) and on a larger scale, like the rest of him. But I've got the Carter Conk, all right. Funny, I used to want to take Dad's name, to be Sky Carter, rather than Sky Smith, but Mum wouldn't have it.

'What are you doing?' asked Grass, pushing open my bedroom door and making me jump. She never remembers to knock, probably because she got so used to sharing a room with me when we were younger. She came in, uninvited, and sat herself down beside me on the bed.

'Nothing,' I said, clumsily trying to hide the photos under my duvet.

Too late. She'd seen them. 'Are you looking at old pictures?'

'Yeah, I guess.'

'Of what?'

'Nothing much. Just stuff from when I was a kid.'

'Are you looking at photos of Dad?' She squashed up closer to me.

'Maybe . . .'

'Can I have a look?' She sounded very curious. 'I don't really remember him at all. I can't see him in my head.' She's only eleven now; she was tiny when he left.

'I guess,' I said, handing over a photo of me sitting on Dad's lap. 'Don't you remember how he used to sing to us?'

She shrugged. 'Not really.' She picked up one of the photos and pulled a face. 'Was he good?'

'Yes, really good. He played in bands. He could play loads of instruments – the guitar, the harmonica, the piano . . .'

'Ocean says he wasn't a nice guy. She hates him.'

'Ocean just thinks whatever Mum says she should think,' I told her. 'He wasn't *all* bad. He was funny and he used to love playing silly games with us. I remember that he'd let us ride around the living room on his back, like he was a horse. And he'd make up stupid songs that rhymed for us.'

She smiled at me. 'Do you think we'll ever see him again?'

'I don't know. Maybe.'

I didn't tell Grass this, but I also clearly remember the last conversation I had with Dad. It was the day before he left for good.

'I'm going away for a while,' he told me. 'On the road.'

'Will you be back soon?'

'Probably,' he lied. 'I'll keep in touch.'

'Will you bring me a present when you come home?'

'Of course I will, Sky-blue. It's a promise.'

Six years later, I'm still waiting.

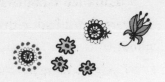

Chapter 5

Bizzie Trip

Today is back to school day. Already. The summer holidays are never long enough. At the start, six weeks seems like forever – days and days of doing whatever you like (if you don't get carted off to Goa against your will, that is), waking up late, seeing your friends – and then, all of a sudden, it's time to go back to school again. Worse, just two days in, it feels like you've never been away.

What's weird is that, even though the holidays go in a flash, people do seem to change over those six weeks. Maybe it's the fresh air or the sunshine, but everyone seems to come back taller. People – boys especially – who came up to your shoulders in the summer term are suddenly the same height as you.

I measured myself when I got up this morning. Over the summer I've grown a total of four centimetres: two in height and two in nose length. To be fair, the amount my nose has grown is just a guess; I've never measured it before today. But it must be *at least* twice as long as it was in July. My beak is now a whopping five and a half centimetres from the middle of my eyebrows, where it starts, to the tip, where it – finally – ends. Then I Googled *nose length* and discovered that for an average European woman, like me, it should be just five point one centimetres. If that's not bad enough, I'm an overachiever in the protrusion stakes too. The average nose sticks out by two point two centimetres; mine is two point three. And we're not even mentioning the bent bit. It's the first time in my life that I've ever wanted to be average at anything. Less is definitely more, when it comes to your nose.

I put the tape measure in my schoolbag, so I could measure Rosie and Vix's noses later this afternoon, when we meet. And then, in desperation, I Googled *ways to make your nose look smaller*. The page I found told me that if I wanted to make my nose look shorter, I should apply my regular foundation all over my face, and then put one shade darker underneath, where my nostrils meet. But I don't have two shades of foundation, just some organic, vegan, tinted moisturiser that Mum bought me for Christmas. I snuck into Ocean's room and 'borrowed' some of hers, painting it on over the top of my base. It looked ridiculous, like I'd accidentally stuck my nose in a cup of hot chocolate and forgotten to wipe it off. I had to wash my face and start all over again. On my second attempt, I used Ocean's bronzer instead, which looked slightly better. Then, as instructed, I defined my eyes with eyeliner to make them look bigger and detract attention away from my nose. I also tried another tip from the article: parting my hair on the side, instead of in the centre. Believe me, that doesn't work when you've got a bob, and a fringe. I made such a mess of my hair that I had to wet it down and blow dry it again. All of which made me late for school. Which wasn't a good way to start the year.

And, frankly, the day has gone downhill from there. I couldn't find my new classroom, got into trouble for being late and had to take a desk right at the front, under the teacher's nose and miles away from Rich. He didn't save me a place next to him, like I hoped he would. Instead, he positioned himself in the back corner, next to Luke. I still haven't had a chance to talk to him about yesterday. I tried last night, but he didn't come online and, when I texted him *Goodnight*, he replied *See you tomorrow*, without even putting a kiss. At breaktime, he played football with his mates.

Now I'm trying to find the GCSE drama room, and I'm lost again.

'Hey, Sky, come over here.'

Here we go, I think. The invitation is from Ella North and it spells trouble. Ella isn't my friend. She's one of those weasly girls who does anything she can find to make herself look more attractive/popular and less boring/stupid. Bitchiness is her MO. She travels around with a coven of girls who are even more weasly than she is and therefore too scared to stand up to her. It's times like these that I wish Rosie and Vix went to the same school as me. When you've got a mum like mine, and a slightly weird name to boot, people like to pick on you. Or try to. It never used to bother me; I'm not your typical victim – I've got tons of friends and a boyfriend, which is more than the bullies have. Usually, I give as good as I get and they soon grow tired and move on to someone else. But I'm not feeling very confident today, what with my worries about my ever-expanding nose and about Rich, and I just want to be left in peace.

'I'm in a hurry,' I say. 'Got somewhere to be.'

'Next period doesn't start for five minutes.'

'Yeah, but . . .'

'Rude, or what?' says Ella, turning to her coven. They all cackle together. 'I only wanted to ask if you had a good summer.'

I offer her my fakest smile. 'It was lovely, thanks. You?'

'Oh yes, mine was fabulous. So have you been on holiday?'

'Yeah, to Goa.'

She smirks. 'Thought so. Must have been *really* sunny there.'

'Duh, it's Goa. It's near the equator. Of course it was sunny.'

'Well, you got a hell of a tan.'

'No I didn't,' I say, lifting up my arm and pushing my

sleeve back. Barely even a watch mark. I'm less than half a shade darker than I usually am because Mum insisted that we smother ourselves in hideous natural sunscreen made from zinc. It made me look like a Goth. 'Not really.'

Ella peers at me, her eyes full of mischief. 'Then why is your nose, like, *bright orange*?'

I contest that. My nose, like the rest of my face, is now almost certainly bright red with embarrassment. Of all the things she could pick on, why did she have to choose my nose? 'No it isn't,' I say, unconvincingly. 'I don't know what you're talking about.' I'm mortified.

Ella reaches into her bag and pulls out a powder compact. 'Yes it is,' she says, smirking, as she clicks it open. 'Look.' She pushes the mirror in front of my face. She's right: over the course of the morning Ocean's bronzing powder has combined with the oils in my skin and transformed to the colour of orangeade. Orangeade now mixed with humiliation. Instead of making my nose look smaller, as I intended, my efforts have made it look twice as obvious. 'Not a good look, Sky, is it, eh? Unless you were going for the "I've been Tangoed" look.'

'I must have rubbed something on it by accident,' I say, feebly. 'I'll go and wash it off.'

'Good idea,' she says. She sounds smug, victorious. 'See you later, Sky.'

I force myself to smile, to make it seem that I'm not bothered. 'Sure.' I turn and walk away as fast as I can, so she can't see that my eyes are brimming with tears.

By the time the final bell rings, I have never, ever been so desperate to see my best friends. I've arranged to meet Vix and Rosie at Starbucks, which is right on the canal by Camden Lock. Now that summer is over, there won't be many more evenings when we can sit outside in the sunshine after school and watch the colourful people of Camden pass by.

'I've had a horrible day,' I say, as we queue for our drinks. 'Please tell me something nice to cheer me up.'

'What's up, Sky?' Vix rubs my arm, affectionately. 'Are you still worrying about what Rich said yesterday?'

'Yeah, that and the fact I had the worst start to the year that you can imagine.'

We sit and I tell them about my bronzing powder disaster, and Ella North, and the fact that Rich hardly said two words to me all day.

'I know just the thing,' says Rosie. 'Remember what I mentioned before, Vix? The thing that Sky would kill to do. Have we got time?'

Vix glances at her phone. 'I reckon so. If we walk fast.' She gets up from her chair, grabbing her half-finished frappuccino and jacket. 'Come on, Sky.'

'Where are we going?' I ask.

'Not telling you,' says Rosie, pulling my chair out from behind me, so I have to get up too. 'It's a surprise. Promise you'll like it though.'

Vix takes one of my arms and Rosie the other, then they lead me a little way up Camden High Street. We cross the road and turn into Hawley Crescent.

'Are we going to the MTV studios?' I ask, excited now.

'We sure are,' says Rosie, 'and hopefully, we're going to see someone who should make you feel a whole lot better.'

'Cool! Who is it?'

'Not telling you! I can't believe you don't know about it already, though. Guess!'

I rack my brains. Rosie likes pop music and guitar bands, while I'm more into R&B and urban music. 'I don't have a clue. It can't be Fieldstar, because they're away on tour . . . Beyoncé?'

'No, much better than that. Well, in your opinion, anyway.'

We've joined a large crowd, which has gathered outside the studios. I search their faces for clues. They don't look like indie kids, or emos. Most of them are around my age, and some of them are really dressed up, like they're going out for the night. I wish I wasn't in my school uniform. Just as I'm about to say, 'I give up', there's a roar from the crowd and someone emerges from the MTV building, surrounded by minders. Rosie shoves me forward and, stumbling, I somehow find myself right at the front of the crowd, staring straight up into the gorgeous features of Bizzie Trip.

'Oh my God!'

I guess I've been so preoccupied with my worries that the news that one of my favourite R&B stars will be up the road

– in person – has completely passed me by. I've been playing his new album nonstop on my iPod for the past month. I know all the words by heart. Especially the rude ones.

Bizzie smiles directly at me and, when I hold out my hand towards him, I'm certain he touches my fingers for just a few more milliseconds than he does everyone else's. I grapple, desperately, with the insides of my school bag to find something for him to sign. All I can find is my GCSE science textbook. It will have to do. He takes it, regards it curiously for a moment, then opens it randomly and scrawls his signature across one of its pages. He just manages to hand it back before he disappears into another section of the crowd.

From now on, for the rest of my life, whenever I remember the formula for copper oxide, I will think of Bizzie Trip.

Feeling light-headed but happy, I find my way back to Rosie and Vix, who are waiting for me at the entrance. 'Thanks so much,' I say, hugging each of my friends in turn. 'I love you two. You're the best. I really don't know what I'd do without you.'

'Yeah, we know,' says Rosie, beaming. 'Hey, you're not so bad yourself.'

I laugh. And then I realise that, for a few minutes at least, I have almost forgotten about my nose. I say 'almost' because, when you've got a nose as big as mine, you can never entirely forget about it. Whichever way you look, you can always see it out of the corner of your eye.

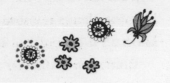

Chapter 6

The Summer Of Love

I'm sitting at my dressing table, carefully applying my make-up for school, when Mum knocks on the door. I can tell it's her because, as always, she gives it three sharp taps. She won't let me have a lock on the door – she doesn't believe we should have any secrets from each other or, even, that being naked is anything to be embarrassed about (cringe). Like most normal people, I don't agree, so, when she started walking in unannounced, I started putting a chair in front of the handle to block her. Then she started worrying about what I might be getting up to in here. '*Are you taking drugs, Sky?*' The knocking thing is our compromise.

'What are you doing?' she says, when it must be pretty

obvious, given that I've got a pot of foundation in one hand and a brush in the other. She glances at her watch. 'Shouldn't you have left for school already? You're going to be late again.'

I tut, irritated by her nagging. 'I'll be quicker if you leave me to it.'

'Why do you need so much make-up for school? Are you even allowed to wear make-up at school? You know you really should let your skin breathe.'

Breathe? What is she going on about? I'm hardly planning to put foundation on from head to toe so that I suffocate, like the woman who was painted gold in that old James Bond film. 'My skin is fine. Don't go on at me, Mum.'

She shrugs. 'I'm just worried about you, Sky. Every time I see you these days you're staring into that mirror. You used to read. You used to make things. You used to care about real issues. Now all you care about is the way you look. What's happened to you, Sky?'

'Nothing,' I say. But her criticism stings. She's right – I never did used to think much about my looks. Now I'm so preoccupied with my nose – whether it's shiny, who can see me in profile, if it's grown – that I barely have time to think about anything else. It's taking me longer and longer to get ready for school. Not that I'm going to admit that to her. 'I've just grown up and got a mind of my own.'

'Growing up doesn't mean you have to become shallow and obsessed with make-up.'

'I'm not shallow! I do still care about important stuff.

Anyway, you care what you look like too,' I counter. 'Otherwise you wouldn't spend money on expensive organic sulphate-free shampoo, cruelty-free make-up and fair-trade hemp clothes in rainbow colours!'

'There's nothing wrong with taking pride in your appearance,' she says, 'but it certainly should not be the only thing you think about.'

'It's not! Besides, I wouldn't have to think about it if I wasn't so hideous! It's not my fault I've got a deformed nose. I need plastic surgery!'

She tuts. 'Don't be ridiculous. Your nose is fine. I think the problem is that you spend too much time looking at unrealistic images in fashion magazines. Those pictures have been airbrushed, you know. Nobody really looks like that.'

Here we go . . . This is one of Mum's favourite lectures. Everything is The Media's fault, apparently. It really grates when she says that – does she think I don't have a mind of my own?

'That's rubbish!' I shout. I'm wound up now. 'Anyway, you're the one who's guilty of airbrushing! You've airbrushed Dad out of our lives. I think the reason you don't want to talk about my nose is because when you look at it, it reminds you of him, and you don't want to think about him.'

'That's not true. Don't be stupid, Sky.'

'Then why won't you ever talk about him? Why don't you have any pictures of him? It's like you're pretending he never existed.'

'No . . . that's not f-f-fair,' she stutters. 'I . . . er, it isn't healthy to dwell on the past. I've never said I wouldn't talk about him if you asked.'

'It doesn't feel that way to me.'

She sighs. 'We haven't got time for this now, Sky. You're late for school. But I promise you that when you get home from school, if there's anything you want to know about him, I'll tell you. OK?'

'Really?' Is she trying to fob me off? Mum doesn't usually lie. And she's never offered anything like this before. So maybe I can trust her.

'Yes, really.'

'OK, Mum. I'll hold you to that,' I say. 'Now let me finish off my make-up, or I really will be late.'

I spend all day at school in a world of my own, dreaming up questions to ask her, things she's never told me about Dad. How and where did she meet him? What made her fall in love with him? Why did they never get married even though they had three kids together? What went wrong? And why, exactly, did Dad leave? I have silly little questions too, about mundane things, the things you should know about people who are important to you. What was Dad's favourite food? Did he like playing sports? Which football team did he support? The more I think about Dad, the more I realise I know virtually nothing about him. All I have are a few snapshots of memories, stuck on a repeat cycle in my mind.

As always, Mum is true to her word (which is probably why she still has such a tiny nose). When I arrive home she makes me a cup of tea and then takes me into the living room, where she's left a pile of old videotapes and a photograph album on the coffee table. I finger them, excitedly, dying to see what's inside.

'I got them out of storage for you,' she says. She seems sad and it makes me feel a bit guilty.

'I don't have to look at them if you don't want me to,' I say, hoping she doesn't agree.

'No, it's all right. It's probably something you should have done years ago.'

'I didn't think you'd kept anything. I thought you'd cleared it all out.' I wonder if I should tell her about the photos I found, the ones she threw away.

'I got rid of a lot of stuff when I was angry, sure. But I've always kept some things – just not out on display.'

'Oh, right.' I decide not to tell her, in case she wants the photos back. They're precious to me. They're mine now. 'So what have you kept, then? What's on the tapes?'

'Footage from your father's gigs, mainly, and a few home movies. It's lucky I never got rid of the old video recorder when we bought the DVD player, isn't it?' she says. 'It still works perfectly. I hate the way technology makes things obsolete these days. It's such a waste.'

'Sure . . . So can I watch them now?'

She nods. I insert a video tape into the machine and Mum

gets up to leave the room. 'Call me if you need anything,' she says. She claims she has things to do but I know that's just an excuse.

The videos aren't labelled, so I watch them in a random order, which means that Dad grows weirdly older, then younger, then older again, with flecks of grey disappearing then reappearing at his temples. The images are really grainy, especially in comparison with the high definition pictures I'm used to. It makes them seem ancient, a world away – although, I suppose, it did all happen in the last century. In the last millennium!

I can't help noticing that I really do look like Dad. It's not just his nose and his dark colouring, but something about his expressions, the way his face crinkles up just like mine when he smiles. Dad seems awkward in front of the camera, happiest and most relaxed when he's on stage, absorbed in his music. He truly can play any instrument. Sometimes he's playing a guitar, sometimes a harmonica or a violin; he's brilliant at them all. I'm also surprised at how pretty Mum was when she was young, and how much Ocean resembles her today. Mum was so fresh-faced and rosy-cheeked, one of those girls who can get away without any make-up at all. Now she has worry lines sketched all over her forehead and ·between her eyes.

When I've been through every tape – some of them twice – I feel sad that there's nothing left to watch. I thumb through the photo album, looking at snaps of Mum and Dad when they were in love – on a beach somewhere in Cornwall, on a barge on a canal, at a music festival. There aren't many photos of Dad with me, Ocean or Grass. Maybe my parents didn't have a good camera then.

'Sky?' Mum is standing at the door. She seems tentative, almost afraid to come in. 'I thought I'd leave you in peace for a while.' I glance at my watch. A whole hour has passed and I haven't realised. 'So have you seen what you wanted to see?'

'Kind of. Thank you. But they're just pictures. I still want to know more about Dad. Like . . .' I rack my brains, trying to remember the questions that have been niggling me all day, in case this is my only opportunity. 'What was he like? Where did you meet him?'

'Well . . .' she begins, sitting herself down beside me on the sofa and launching into what sounds like a well-rehearsed speech. She doesn't go into much detail; she talks as if she's been expecting this moment, my questions, for years. She looks down while she speaks, her voice emotionless and monotone. This is what she tells me.

She met Dad in 1988 at a 'Summer of Love' music festival – a giant rave in a field that lasted for three days. It was supposed to recreate the 'Summer of Love' in the Sixties, when everybody was a hippy, just like Mum. She's always said she was born in the wrong era. There were thousands of people there, but as soon as she spotted Dad, that was it. She didn't notice anybody else. She was nineteen and on her gap year, there to sell food from a stall; he was thirty and hanging out with his musician friends. She glossed over the next part, when they 'got together', but I think she was a bit of a groupie, following him around the country, helping his band sell CDs at their gigs. She genuinely thought he was going to be the next big thing, because he was so talented and handsome. Most of all, he was a free spirit and that was what attracted her to him. Her parents – my grandparents – were stuffy and strict and didn't understand her. But he seemed to 'get' her.

They fell in love and eventually settled down in a flat in Camden (not in our flat, which she bought later with money from an inheritance). Renting in Camden was a lot cheaper then, but it was still tough to manage. She found a job working in a vegetarian café and he played gigs. He hardly ever got up before noon, didn't make much money, and spent a lot of what he did make on alcohol. Worse, drinking made him unpredictable, and nasty, sometimes. He was away a lot, and Mum had to cope alone, even when she was pregnant. By the time she realised she was living with a penniless alcoholic, who'd never change, she had three young children, and she was stuck. She wouldn't take help from her parents because she didn't want all the 'we told you so's, and so she managed as best she could.

Then, one day, Dad went out on the road again and, this time, he didn't come home. He phoned her from a payphone and said he'd met someone else, someone who didn't 'nag him all the time about money and drinking'. Mum was devastated; then she toughened up. She says she realised that she didn't need him any more and, more surprisingly, she didn't even want him. The rest I already know: gradually, he stopped phoning us and sending presents and cards, until he vanished from our lives forever. And after that, she tells me, we all lived happily ever after. I'm surprised she doesn't finish with 'The End'.

'Oh!' I say, when she's finished. It's all I can manage. 'Oh.' The way she's described Dad doesn't chime with my memories of him at all. He was fun and kind and generous too, but she hasn't mentioned any of that. Surely she's exaggerated the bad parts – I can't remember things ever being *that* awful.

I'm now absolutely certain that, despite everything she's said, I still want to get to know him for myself.

'I really appreciate everything you've told me, but it's not enough. I need to see him again. Will you help me find him, Mum? Please?'

She pauses and takes a deep breath. 'I was praying you wouldn't ask that. No, I'm sorry. That's one thing I can't do. Not even for you.'

I should have known she'd say that but, somehow, I wasn't expecting it. She's been so sweet today. 'Why not, Mum? It's really important to me.'

'I just can't,' she says, quietly. 'Not because I don't love you and want to make you happy, but because I really don't think it's a good idea. He'll only let you down, Sky. It's better to hold on to your good memories. If you meet up with him again he'll only disappoint you. I learnt that lesson many times.'

'But maybe he's changed. Maybe he'll be a good dad now. Maybe he wants to get in touch but doesn't know how to.'

'He knows where we are,' she says. 'We haven't moved from Camden. He could have written any time.'

'Yeah, but maybe he thinks we all hate him. Like you do.'

She shrugs. 'I don't hate him, Sky. I just know that having him back in our lives again isn't a good idea. We've all moved on and we're much happier now.'

Again! She keeps saying we're all so happy now. Can't she see it's not true? She might be happy, but I'm not. 'So you won't help me?'

'No, I'm sorry. I can't help you.'

'Thanks a lot, Mum.' I can't look at her. I feel tearful and angry.

She tries to stroke my hand, but I won't let her. 'It's just too painful for me, Sky. And I don't want you to get hurt.'

'Not seeing him is hurting me too. Can't you see that?'

She looks pained. 'That's because you don't know what he's really like. I can't stop you, Sky, if you're determined to find him. I won't stop you. It's just not a good idea.'

'Fine,' I say, getting up from the sofa. 'I'll do it on my own, then.'

I sound confident, but I'm not. I don't want to do it on my own. I want Mum to help me. It hurts that she won't. I have this image in my head of us all sitting around the table together, having dinner, hearing Dad's stories, catching up on the last few years. We're all happy again. I'm not naive enough to think my parents will get back together, but can't they at least be friends? Mum's all about love and forgiveness when it suits her; why is she such a hypocrite when it comes to Dad?

Chapter 7

The Dad Detectives

The first person I call is Rich. I'm dying to tell him about how I've decided to hunt for Dad and, who knows, he might be able to help. Most of all, I really need a hug.

'Hey, babe,' he says. 'What's up?'

'It's too complicated to explain over the phone. Will you come round?'

'What for?'

To see me, obviously. To spend time with me. Because you're my boyfriend, and that's what boyfriends do. 'Um . . . I wanted to talk to you about something.'

There's that bristle again. 'Right . . . About what?'

'Come round and I'll tell you.'

'Right now? We're seeing each other tomorrow night anyway.'

I am seeing him tomorrow night, it's true, for our anniversary dinner. But this can't wait. 'If you can. Please. Unless you've got something better to do.'

'Well . . .' he begins and I know he's trying to decide whether football on TV or his new computer game count as 'something better'. 'I guess I can pop round for a few minutes. If you really want me to.'

'Thanks,' I say, before he can change his mind. 'See you in five.'

I hang up and go to my dressing table to redo my make-up and brush my hair. I don't think my nose has grown too much this week; maybe – fingers crossed – it's reaching a plateau. I look tired, though, a bit puffy-eyed. I had a good cry earlier, after Mum said she wouldn't help. I came up to my room and lay on my bed, and the tears just came. I haven't cried for ages, not great big, salty, snotty tears like that. I wonder if Dad has ever cried, thinking about me and Ocean and Grass.

I hear the buzz of the intercom but, before I can get to the entry phone to open the downstairs door, Mum has already let Rich in. I should have told her he was coming. They'll be making awkward small talk now, about school and how Rich's parents are, and how the whole family should come for tea, which will never, ever happen. I hear him squeaking across the hall floorboards towards my bedroom, in the half-size too big trainers we bought a few weeks ago. I stand by the door, ready to greet him.

He pushes the door open and bounces into my room on his air soles. 'So what's going down?'

'Eh?' I'd have liked a kiss hello. I move towards him and he gives me a quick peck on the lips.

'Why did you drag me round here? What's happening?'

'I didn't drag you. Anyway . . . it's about my dad . . .'

Rich sits down on my bed, so I sit next to him. Our knees are touching, but he doesn't put his arm around me. 'I thought you didn't have a dad,' he says. 'I thought he'd died or something, when you were a kid.'

'He didn't die,' I say, irritated. I *know* I've told Rich the whole story once before. 'He walked out on us and never came back. And then he disappeared.'

'So you don't know where he is?'

'Exactly. That's why I wanted to talk to you. I want to find him.' I tell Rich about my conversation with Mum and the videos I've watched. Now I need a hug more than ever. I lean my head on Rich's shoulder and he pats my hair, unromantically, the way you'd pet a dog.

'I don't get why you want to see him. He sounds like a loser.'

'Because he's my dad. The only one I'll ever have.'

Rich shrugs. 'OK, fair enough. If that's what you want to do, go for it.'

'Thanks.' I'm waiting for him to volunteer to help me, but he doesn't. 'So will you help me?'

'Sure, if you want. Not sure what I can do though. I don't even know what he looks like.'

Nor do I, I think. Not any more. 'I know, but . . . Anyway, can I have a hug?'

'Course,' he says. He twists around so that he's facing me and puts his arms around my shoulders, pulling me in towards him. He smells a bit sweaty but I don't mind too much. The hug turns into a snog, which isn't really what I want right now, but I let myself go with it. I do like kissing Rich.

There are three sharp taps on the door. Rich jumps away from me, as if he's had an electric shock. I don't know why; one thing about having a mum like mine is that she's very laid-back about things like snogging. She says she trusts me.

'Hey, guys,' says Mum, poking her head around the door. She's trying to be cool again. I cringe. She attempts to make eye contact with me but I'm still upset with her so I look away. 'Um, would you like to stay for supper, Rich? There's plenty to go around.'

'No, thanks,' he says, clambering up from the bed and smoothing down his jeans. 'I'd better be going, actually. See you at school tomorrow, Sky?'

'Um, yeah,' I say. I don't feel that our conversation is finished yet. 'Talk later, maybe?'

'OK.' He gives me another peck, this time on the cheek, and then he's off, squeaking down the hall again.

I'm quiet and sulky during dinner, especially as I'm not in the least bit hungry. Grass wants to know what's wrong with me. I tell her I've got a headache. I think Mum has already talked things over with Ocean because she gives me a disapproving look. I give her one back. I push my food around my plate, eat a few mouthfuls and then announce that I have coursework to do, so I'm going to my room. Mum sighs and nods but she doesn't stop me.

I do have coursework to do but I have no intention of doing it straight away. Instead, I go on Facebook and message Rosie and Vix. I might not be able to count on my mum or my boyfriend to help me find Dad. But I know I can count on my best friends.

Will you come over? I type. *I've got something important I need to ask you.*

They both message back almost immediately. *What is it?* writes Rosie. *Sounds exciting!*

Course I will, hon, says Vix. *Are you OK?*

That really sums up the difference between my two best friends. Rosie's all about having fun, while Vix worries about everyone and wants to take care of them. I couldn't manage without either of them. I don't know why I didn't call them earlier, instead of Rich.

I ask them if they'll come over in an hour, which should give me just enough time to do a bit of homework first. I'm so lucky that we all live on Paradise Avenue and can pop in and out of each other's homes as often as we like (parents permitting). It's almost like having sisters – ones you'd choose, not the ones you're lumbered with.

They turn up together and I usher them into my room before Mum can get her claws into them. Neither of them can stay more than an hour; it's a school night and already past eight. I quickly bring them up to speed on what's happened.

'You've never told us much about your dad before,' says Vix. 'I never thought to ask.'

'That's because there isn't much to tell,' I say, filling them in on my scant memories and the little I do know. 'I need to find him to figure out the rest.'

'Of course we'll help you,' says Rosie, and Vix nods in agreement. Rosie gets on really well with her dad. Even though he embarrasses her sometimes, he's fun and sweet and easy to talk to. She totally gets why I want to find my father. 'It'll be fun. We can be like private detectives.'

Vix is a little more concerned. 'What if he turns out to be a waste of space, like your mum says? Or worse, what if he doesn't even want to meet you?'

I shrug. I haven't considered the possibility that he won't want to see me. 'I'm sure he will. Anyway, he might have changed. He might have stopped drinking now. And maybe he acted the way he did because he wasn't happy with my mum. It can't be all his fault. I know she can be a pain to live with sometimes.'

A flicker of annoyance passes across Vix's face. 'Your mum's cool, Sky. A bit out there and eccentric, but she's sweet.'

'Yeah, I know. Sometimes,' I say, guiltily. I suddenly see things through Vix's eyes. Here I am slagging Mum off, but I'm lucky to have her. Vix's mum is ill a lot. She can't go out much or take Vix anywhere. Vix has to do a lot of the work around her house too. It's probably why she's more serious and grown up than me or Rosie.

'Anyway,' says Rosie. 'You won't know what he's like until you meet him. So where do we start?'

'The internet,' I say. 'Where else?'

All three of us crowd around my PC. I have butterflies. Maybe, in just a few clicks, I'll be able to track down my dad. I wonder why I've never thought to look him up before. It's such an obvious thing to do.

'Do you think he might be on Facebook?' says Vix.

'God, I hope not. He's way too old,' I say. Mum has been threatening to join up for months, not because she wants to spy on me, like most mums would, but because she likes my friends and wants to keep in touch with them. I've told her that if she does join I won't let her friend me. 'Worth a try though . . .'

'What's his name then?' Rosie already has her hands poised above the keyboard.

'Connor Carter.'

'Cool name,' says Vix.

'Yeah, way better than Smith.'

'Or Buttery,' says Rosie, although, secretly, I think she likes her weird name. 'OK . . . C-O-N-N-O-R C-A-R-T-E-R . . . Is that right?'

I nod and she presses return.

'God, Sky, there are hundreds of them! It must be a really popular name.'

'Great,' I say. 'I guess we'd better trawl through them all then. Shouldn't take too long; with the ones that have pictures it should be obvious.'

It's a dead end. Even though half the men on Facebook seem to be called Connor Carter, not one of them could be my father. I guess that would have been too easy. He doesn't have a MySpace page either, or appear to belong to any social networking sites. That's what comes of being old, I suppose.

'What next?' says Rosie. 'Shall we just Google him?'

I frown. 'I guess. God, it would have been so much easier if my mum would help. She must know the names of the bands he was in. Try, *Connor Carter, music* or something. Or *Connor Carter, musician*.'

'OK,' says Rosie. 'Here goes . . .' She presses return and, in an instant, there's a long list of suggested links which may, or may not, feature my dad. We scroll down the pages, working our way through them, ignoring the ones which definitely aren't him (about college kids in America, for example) and clicking on the ones that just might be. It's a frustrating process: Dad seems to have left as little trace on the internet as he has in my life.

I'm almost ready to admit defeat when we find something.

'Look!' says Vix. 'Is that him?' She points her finger at a link about some gig, somewhere, which lists one Connor Carter among the musicians playing.

'Go on! Click on it!'

The band – featuring Connor Carter on violin – was called The Four Horsemen. The gig was at a venue in South London. It was five years ago.

'It's something, I suppose,' says Vix. 'Let's bookmark it.'

'OK.' I feel flat. This is going to be harder than I imagined. 'Is there anything else?'

Our search reveals a few more Four Horsemen gigs, with no photos and no further details. And then, about three years ago, the trail dries up. 'The Four Horseman must have split,' I say. 'Oh well, it was worth a shot.'

Vix puts her arm on my shoulder. 'Never mind, hon. There must be another way.'

Rosie looks thoughtful. Then she practically leaps into the air. 'I know!' she says, sounding extremely pleased with herself. 'I've got an ace idea. Why don't we go to Dot's Music Shop and ask there? It's just up the road, on St Pancras Way. Rufus Justice told me about it! It's where all the musicians in Camden get their guitar strings and their music and stuff. It's been there for years. If your dad ever lived and played in Camden, they're bound to know about him!'

'That's a great idea!' I say, excited again. 'Let's check it out on Saturday.'

Chapter 8

A Date
With Disaster

Rich and I are in Strada, an Italian restaurant on Parkway. It's not the most romantic place in the world (all the tables are close together), but the food is tasty and at least it's a proper restaurant. Rich has never taken me to a proper restaurant before, only to KFC or to Burger King. I have a sneaking suspicion that tonight might have been his mum's idea, but I'm not going to ask because I'd rather not know. Sometimes, I get the feeling Rich's mum likes me more than he does.

Rich didn't remember that our anniversary was coming up – I had to tell him – but Rosie says boys never do remember that kind of detail so, for once, I shouldn't hold it against him. And, although six months is ages, it's not strictly an anniversary, just a half one, so he might not have realised its significance. It doesn't matter now; he agreed to go out for dinner to celebrate and even said he'd pay. I think he's trying to make things better between us.

I check my watch. Nine p.m. Six months ago, at precisely this time, we were at Jessica Carrington's fourteenth birthday party, snogging each other's faces off, and I had never felt so happy. I wonder if I should mention it? Jog Rich's memory? Maybe it would make the atmosphere between us more romantic. I glance at him; he has chocolate sauce stuck in the crevices at the corners of his mouth. I think better of it. Tonight things are . . . different. But at least we're out together, just the two of us, without his mates.

It's been an OK evening, I guess. We've talked a bit, although not about anything important, like how my hunt for Dad is going. He hasn't asked. We've eaten garlic bread and pizza and now Rich is working his way through a chocolate pudding, while I sip mint tea. 'So,' he's saying, 'we're playing them next week and if I score then I might be captain. Cool, eh?'

'Yeah . . . sure . . . That's great . . .'

He's rambling on about how he's better playing on the left side, and I have no idea what he's talking about. I can't concentrate. A woman has just walked into the restaurant and sat down at the table opposite. All I can do is stare at her profile. I'm transfixed. She has the most enormous, hooked nose that I've ever seen. It's quite astonishingly big. Wow! I can't take my eyes off it. I really don't understand how she can dare to go out in public with a nose like that. Unless . . . I look to her side. No, there's no sign of a white stick or a guide dog. She must know what's protruding from the middle of her face. But she seems oblivious to it, smiling and chatting with her friend, as if she doesn't have a care in the world. She has made-up eyes and glossy hair, and she's wearing a lovely tan leather jacket and silk scarf, so she clearly cares about her appearance. So why hasn't she got rid of that nose? She must be at least thirty. Doesn't she mind it? Has she just got used to it?

'Rich . . .' I begin, cautiously. He's already told me he's fed up with me going on about my nose and I've managed to avoid the subject all night, so far. But now I can't help myself. 'Is my nose as big as hers?' I nod towards the woman, as subtly as I can.

'Sorry? What?'

I lower my voice, to make sure she can't hear me. 'I asked you if my nose is as big as that woman's. Her, over there, with the blond hair.'

'Eh?' He sighs. 'I was talking about the match. I knew you weren't listening.'

'I was listening, honestly. I just got distracted, sorry. So is it?'

'What?'

'As big? Or bigger even? Just tell me quickly.'

He sighs again and, a bit too obviously, cranes his neck so he can see the woman. Then he tuts. 'Don't be stupid, Sky. Your nose is nothing like hers. No way. Don't start on about your nose again.'

'Really? Did you look properly? Are you saying mine isn't that big?'

'Course not.'

I feel reassured for a second, but then I start to doubt him. 'Hmm. I bet people tell her that too, all the time.'

He shrugs. 'Yeah, well she looks like she isn't bothered about her nose. So nor should you be. Anyway, as I was saying, if I play down the left I reckon I should be a dead cert to score next week . . .'

Maybe she's not bothered about her nose because she's clocked me and she knows that hers isn't as big as mine. Do people stare at my profile in restaurants and pity me too? Oh my God, is that what she's talking with her friend about? Is that why she's smiling and laughing? Is she wondering how Rich could possibly fancy me? I scan the room for noses. It's amazing how many shapes and sizes they come in, from wide, squishy ones, to long ones with square nostrils, to baby ones that are so cute and perfectly defined that they look like they've been stolen from dolls' heads. Is mine the biggest in the whole room? In the whole of Camden? In the whole of Britain?

'What about hers?' I gesture towards another woman, who has a slightly beaky nose.

Rich barely glances at her. 'Jeez, Sky, this is really boring now. No, your nose isn't like hers. You've got a different shaped face.'

'Different . . . God, that's just a diplomatic way of saying my nose is as big as hers, isn't it?'

'No, it's just completely different.'

'Different in a . . . bigger way?'

He looks really annoyed now. To tell the truth, I'm starting to annoy myself. 'I can't win, can I?' he says. 'If I tell you your nose isn't as big, you think that I'm lying. But if I say it's the same size or bigger, you'll hate me and get even more paranoid and fixated. Please stop asking me.'

We sit in silence for a minute, staring sulkily at each other over the candle. At least I know the answer now: my nose is just as big as the other woman's. And I can't trust Rich to give me a straight answer.

'Last question, I promise,' I say, hesitantly. I really can't stop until I know the answer. 'Then I'll shut up about it . . .' I take a deep breath. 'Would you fancy me more if I had a smaller nose?'

Rich rolls his eyes. 'Sky, I never even noticed your nose until you started going on and on about it when you got home from Goa. I've always thought you were really pretty. But talking about your nose all the time, acting paranoid and insecure like you are, is a total turn-off. I've had enough now. It's dead boring. It's making you dead boring. So, if you really hate your nose that much, then why don't you stop moaning about it and do something – like get it fixed – instead?'

It couldn't hurt more if he'd punched me right on the nose. 'Fine!' I spit, no longer caring if anyone can hear me. I feel upset and angry but, most of all, I feel vindicated. Rich wouldn't have told me to do something about my nose if he didn't think I needed to, would he? As soon as I get home I'm going to start looking into plastic surgery. 'Do you know what?' I say. I make it sound like a threat. 'Maybe I will.'

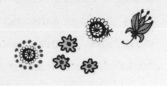

Chapter 9

Cut It Off, Now!

I set my alarm early on Saturday morning, even though I've barely slept. Today is an important day and my usual weekend lie-in can wait until tomorrow. Later, I'm meeting Rosie and Vix to go to Dot's Music Shop. But first, I have something else to do, something that can't wait.

My doctor's surgery is in a swanky, modern health centre just off Kentish Town Road, about ten minutes' walk from my flat. I've never been here alone before, and I feel nervous as I walk through the sliding doors. I don't like doctors' surgeries; they're full of sick people. Not that I've been here more than a handful of times. Mum prefers to take us to the homeopathic doctor, or the Chinese medicine place on

Camden High Street. She says modern drugs are full of toxins and make you sicker than you were to start with.

I march up to the reception desk, trying to look both confident and wan at the same time. Which isn't easy, especially with the amount of bronzer I've applied to my nose to shade it. The receptionist is staring at a computer screen and barely glances at me. 'Can I see a doctor please? Now?' I ask.

'Do you have an appointment? Saturday mornings are by appointment only.'

'No. Erm... The thing is, I couldn't call from home and I don't have any credit on my phone.'

'What's the problem? Is it an emergency?'

'I'd rather not say. Yes, it's sort of an emergency.' After I came home from the restaurant last night, I did lots of reading on the internet and, while I know they probably can't give me a nose job here and now, in my local GP's surgery, I also know that the sooner I get this started, the better.

'Name?' she barks. 'Address? Date of birth?'

'Er . . .' I'm flustered. 'Sky Smith. Er, 2B Verlaine Court, Paradise Avenue. Fourteenth of January. Er, I'm fourteen. Nearly fifteen.'

'Right. I've found your notes. OK. You can see Dr Buttery. There's a couple of people ahead of you.'

'Oh,' I say, disappointed. I really don't want to see Rosie's mum. 'Can't I see someone else?'

'Nah, sorry. She's the only doctor on duty today. Like I

said, it's appointment only. I can make you an appointment with your own GP for another day – say, next Wednesday?'

'No . . . I've got school . . . I can't wait till then.'

'Then I'm afraid it's Dr Buttery, or nothing.'

I nod. 'OK, I guess.' Maybe I should just go home and come back another time. Then again, doctors aren't allowed to judge you, or tell your mum stuff, are they? I don't want to take the risk, but I can't face delaying this either. 'OK, I'll see her.'

'Take a seat in the waiting area. We'll call you when she's ready.'

I walk to the bench furthest from the other patients, and sit on the edge. There's a bunch of really old magazines on the table, and I leaf through them, checking out last year's fashions. Of course, all the models have beautiful, straight noses, just like they do every season. Big, ugly noses are never en vogue (or in *Vogue*). And it's not down to airbrushing, whatever Mum says. At the back of one magazine is a directory jam-packed with adverts for plastic surgery clinics. I had no idea there were so many. When I'm sure nobody's looking, I tear the pages out of the magazine and stuff them into my pocket. Waiting is making me feel agitated. I want to get this over with.

'Sky Smith . . . Sky Smith . . .' There's my name over the tannoy. I feel a pang of nerves and stand up. 'Please go to room 3B.'

I walk through the waiting area, aware that everyone is

watching me, wondering what I'm here for. Some of them must be seeing me in profile. I cringe, and bend my head forward. I'm starting to regret chopping my long hair off now. Having a fringe is the worst thing you can do when you've got a big nose. Why didn't the hairdresser warn me?

1B . . . 2B . . . 3B . . . I take a deep breath and rap on the door. A few seconds pass and then I hear Dr Buttery say, 'Come in,' in exactly the same tone she uses when I go round to her house to see Rosie. I peer my head around, then walk in slowly.

She seems surprised to see me. 'Ah, Sky. I didn't know you were coming. So what can I do for you?'

I would have thought that was obvious; can't she tell just by looking at me? Can't *everyone* tell?

'Um, you know, it's kind of embarrassing. I need . . . I'm not sure where to start. I need help with something. I've got to do something about it now . . . I can't wait any longer.'

She beckons me to sit down and take off my jacket. 'There's no need to be embarrassed, Sky, I'm a doctor. Anything you say in here won't go any further.'

'I know . . . it's just . . . you're Rosie's mum.'

'Not at work, I'm not. Here, I'm just Dr Buttery. Right. Good. Well, first of all, Sky, you are under sixteen. I *am* allowed to see you alone, but I'd rather your mother were here.'

'Oh no, she wouldn't come. She doesn't approve.'

'Have you spoken to her about this?'

'Yes, and she told me not to be so stupid and to forget about it. She said I'm way too young and that if I still want to do it when I'm older, then I can think about it then.'

Dr Buttery frowns. My mum and Rosie's mum aren't exactly friends. They're total opposites. Rosie's mum is the most sensible woman on the planet and she doesn't have any time for my mum's chanting and alternative medicine and herbal remedies. They had an argument once, when Mum said she didn't want me to get a vaccine at school because she was worried about the side effects. Rosie's mum said she was being irresponsible. I have a suspicion that Rosie's mum thinks my mum isn't a very good mother.

'That attitude won't help anyone,' she says, 'because you'll just go ahead and do it anyway, won't you?'

'Exactly,' I say. 'I knew a doctor would understand.'

'OK, well, I'm happy to discuss it with you, as you're being so sensible. But you are only fourteen. Too young, really.'

'I know, but it's been bothering me for ages. I *have* to do something about it. Promise you won't tell her?'

'No, legally I don't have to. But I'd rather *you* did.'

'OK, I promise,' I say, crossing my fingers to guard against the nose-expanding effects of my lie.

'Right, so let's discuss your options. I'd hate for you to get into trouble. I know you have a serious, long-term boyfriend.'

What's Rich got to do with this? 'Yes, I do . . . But we're sort of on the rocks . . . We've been arguing a lot. I think it's partly because of my, er, problem.'

'Sky, you should never, ever do anything just to keep a boy. It has to be your decision.'

'Oh, it is. It's totally my choice.'

'It's your body. You decide what to do with it and when.'

'Yes, absolutely. But I don't think he likes it. He wants me to get rid of it.'

She raises her eyebrows, as if she disapproves, and sighs. 'All right, then. I'll help you because that's the responsible thing to do. But remember, it's still important to be safe, to use some sort of protection. I'll give you a leaflet before you leave. There are all kinds of diseases out there, you know.'

'Oh, you mean like a face mask? To stop germs getting in?'

She peers at me, quizzically. 'Yes, a bit like that. I'm surprised and rather concerned that they haven't taught you about this at your school. The leaflet will tell you all you need to know.'

'Thanks.'

'OK, so there are several different options. Have you had any thoughts about what you want? What would suit you best? Injection, implant, pill . . . ?'

'Eh, sorry, but what did you say?' I stare at her open-mouthed. An injection? A pill? What is she on about? I know science has progressed lately, but even I know that, sadly, they haven't yet developed a pill to make your nose shrink, Alice in Wonderland style.

'I was just explaining your options,' she says. 'The pill doesn't suit everyone.'

Oh my God! I cringe so hard I'm surprised she can't see it. Now I understand — and I really wish I didn't. She's talking about *the* pill. She thinks I want to go on the pill. I can feel my face flushing. 'No, sure, but . . .' I begin, unsure how to carry on. This is *so* embarrassing. I didn't think it was possible to be more embarrassed about anything than I am about my nose. I guess I was wrong. 'I . . . I . . .'

But she isn't listening. She's gone into autopilot (or rather, doctor) mode. 'Right, well, whatever we choose, the first thing I need to do is take your blood pressure.'

'Um, oh, OK. It's just that . . .' Try as I might, I can't find the words.

She swivels around in her chair and takes something out of a drawer. 'Roll up your sleeve and make a fist.'

I sigh and decide to let her do it, anyway. I've never had my blood pressure done before and I'm quite curious about it. And, frankly, giving her my arm is a lot easier than trying to correct our misunderstanding. She attaches a black cuff to my arm and plugs a wire into it. The other end is attached to a little machine. Then she presses a button on the machine and the cuff begins to squeeze my arm, tighter and tighter. It grips so hard that it hurts. Still, this must be less painful than having bits of my nose shaved off.

'Good,' she says, approvingly, and the air deflates from the cuff, freeing my arm. I rub it. 'So have you thought about what you'd like to try?'

'The thing is . . . I, er, I don't . . . want . . . the pill or, er, any of them,' I manage to say. 'I'm actually here about an operation.'

'An *operation*? Isn't that a little drastic?'

'Yes, maybe it is. But, um, I don't think there's any other way to make my nose smaller. You know — they can shave a bit off, so it's straighter and not so beaky.'

Dr Buttery's face changes. The serious look disappears, then, as if she's unable to stop herself, she starts chortling. She might even be choking. 'Sky,' she begins, when she can finally form some words, 'tell me again, what exactly are we talking about here?'

I feel suddenly self-conscious. I don't like drawing attention to my problem. 'My nose, of course. I was trying to tell you, but . . .'

'Your *nose*?' She can hardly breathe for laughing. It feels like she's laughing at my nose, even though I know she isn't. I don't think I've ever seen her laugh before, so this is really quite unnerving. She's shaking so much I think she's going to fall off her chair. 'I thought . . . I thought . . . that you wanted contraceptive advice.'

I cringe again. 'I know you did! God, no! I don't! No way! I'm here because I want a nose job. A rhino-wotsit. You know.'

'I'm so sorry, Sky,' says Dr Buttery, clearing her throat. 'I just assumed. From what you said. I never actually asked, did I? That's terribly unprofessional of me. Right, your nose.' Another giggle escapes. She clears her throat again.

'It's not funny,' I say. I feel like crying. 'My nose isn't funny. It's deformed. Hideous.'

Dr Buttery finally seems to get a grip on herself. She stares at me, her eyes flickering as she scans my face from top to bottom. 'Sky, dear, there's really nothing wrong with your nose. It's a perfectly normal nose.'

'No, it's not. It's ugly and huge and wonky, and I want rid of it.'

'Really, it's in perfect proportion. It suits your face.'

'That's what everyone says. To make me feel better. I thought at least a doctor would be honest.'

She sighs. 'I really don't see how I can help you, Sky. Can you breathe through it OK?'

I nod. My eyes are brimming with tears.

'Has it been broken in an accident?'

I shake my head.

'Then really, Sky, there's nothing I can do for you. You don't need surgery. Your mum is right: give yourself time to get used to it. Wait a few years. You can make a decision when you're older. But, until then, no reputable surgeon will touch your nose. You're still growing, after all. It will probably be fully grown by the time you're sixteen, seventeen, or so.'

STILL GROWING? *STILL GROWING!* No way! So my nose *is* going to grow even bigger? I've got to wait until it's even larger? How much larger? That's the worst possible thing she could have told me. Ever.

'O-Oh,' I stutter.

'We could chat about counselling if you'd like. Maybe you'd like to talk to someone about how you feel. It seems to me that the problem is in your head.'

My problem isn't *in* my head, it's *on* my head! 'I don't want counselling, I want a new nose,' I say. I get up and grab my jacket so fast that my chair tips back. Dr Buttery catches it.

'Sky . . .' she begins. 'Let's talk about this. Stop . . .' But I've already closed the door behind me and fled into the corridor.

What did she say? No reputable surgeon would touch my nose? She must be wrong. I'm just going to have to try to find one for myself.

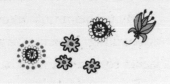

Chapter 10

Has Anybody Seen
A Lost Dad?

I set out to meet Rosie and Vix on the corner of our street at three, just as we've arranged. As I walk down Paradise Avenue, I feel distracted. Although I've had time to calm down since the doctor's appointment, my head is chock full of finding Dad and getting my nose fixed and worrying about the way things are with Rich. My brains are in such a mush that I'm not sure which of my worries is the most important, or even if they're each just one part of the same big problem: my mess of a life.

My friends are both there, waiting for me, when I arrive, and it cheers me to see them. We kiss each other and, as we walk, catch up on the morning's gossip. We've already texted and messaged each other, so there isn't much news to report. They've told me what they think of Rich following our disastrous anniversary dinner, and I'm sure they'll bring it up again over coffee, later. I haven't told them about my visit to the doctor yet. First things first . . .

Dot's Music Shop is tucked away behind Kentish Town Road and Camden Road, on a corner facing a little grass-covered traffic island with an old, red telephone box. I've walked past it many times, but I've never been inside. You can hardly see through the windows for all the posters and pictures pasted up on them, and the guitars that hang enticingly behind, just out of reach. Even the steps are painted black and white, like piano keys.

'Do you know what?' says Rosie, pausing at the bottom of the steps. 'I think I might have been here before, when I was a kid. I think my mum brought me here to buy a recorder.'

Vix giggles. 'You can buy another one now if you like.'

I'm too stressed to chat about recorders. 'Here goes,' I say to my friends. I take a deep breath and lean against the front door. It opens with a pleasing, old-fashioned tinkle.

'Hello, girls, what can I do for you?' asks a kind-looking woman, with rosy cheeks and greying hair, who must be Dot.

Hesitantly, I walk up to the counter, with Rosie and Vix on either side of me. 'Um, we, er, don't need to buy anything. Sorry. We just wanted some help.' I'm flustered and not quite sure where to start. Asking someone to help you find your long lost dad isn't quite the same as asking if they've seen your missing cat.

Rosie steps forward. 'She wants to find her dad. She wonders if you can help.'

'Her *dad*?'

'Yes, he's a musician,' explains Vix. 'He used to live in Camden and play gigs here too. She hasn't seen him for years.'

'Right,' says Dot. She looks intrigued. I guess this isn't the type of request she gets every day. She smiles at me. 'And how can I help?'

'We thought you might know him,' says Rosie. She clears her throat, which is what she always does when she's about to name-drop someone famous. 'My friend Rufus Justice from Fieldstar – he lives next door – told me know you all the musicians in Camden.'

Dot laughs. 'Ah, Rufus, yes. He comes in sometimes. But I don't know about *all* of them.' She makes eye contact with me. 'So what's your dad's name? Sorry, what's *your* name? I'm Dot.'

'Hi Dot. I'm Sky, and this is Vix and Rosie,' I say, nodding towards my friends. 'My dad is called Connor Carter. He lived in Camden until about six years ago. I think he might have been in a band called The Four Horsemen. I don't know much else. He was Irish. Oh, and he played loads of different instruments, so maybe he came in for strings or music, or something.'

Dot furrows her brow, concentrating hard. I think she's

trying to work out if she remembers Connor Carter, or The Four Horsemen. 'It doesn't ring a bell,' she says. 'I'm sorry.'

'Oh.' I'm disappointed. Then I remember the photograph I have folded up in my pocket. 'I have a picture. Do you want to see it?'

'Sure.' I pass it to her and she studies it for a minute.

'He looks a lot like you.'

I blush. She means the nose. 'I know.'

'But I don't recognise him, I'm afraid. He might not have come in here, or I might never have seen his band play.'

'He might have been in other bands, I think, but I don't know their names.'

'Her mum won't help,' Rosie pipes up. 'She doesn't want Sky to find him.'

I nudge her. 'Too much information,' I whisper.

Dot looks like she feels sorry for me. 'Hmm. Another thought. He might be a member of something called the Musicians' Union. I have a directory in the back here ... hang on.' She goes behind the counter and bends down for a moment, re-emerging with a battered, old book. 'Right, let's have a look. Carter. C. Hmm ...'

I crane my neck so I can see what she's reading. It's a long list of names and addresses. Carey. Carson ... I scroll down them, following her finger with my eyes.

'There's a few Carters, but no Connor. Are you sure he didn't use any other name?'

'I'm not sure,' I say, again acutely aware of how little I

know about my dad. 'I don't think so.'

Dot must sense my disappointment. She smiles kindly and says, 'I'm sorry, love, he's not here.' She snaps the book shut and replaces it behind the counter. 'It just means he isn't a member. Not everybody joins.'

'Right.' I stand awkwardly, shifting from foot to foot, unsure what to say or do next. I guess it's time to thank Dot and leave. Another dead end. Vix gives me a sympathetic smile and takes my arm. Rosie must have grown bored, because she's gone to the front of the shop, where she's rifling through a stand of sheet music.

'I tell you what,' says Dot. 'I can put a note in the window for you if you like.' She points to a board displaying adverts for concerts, guitar lessons and everything else related to music in Camden. 'You never know, someone might spot it and get in touch.'

'Really? Like a missing person's poster? Would you do that for me? That would be fantastic. Thank you.'

Dot sticks Dad's picture to a blank, A4 sheet and then, underneath it, we write a note together. It reads, *If anyone has any information on the whereabouts of musician Connor Carter, formerly of bands including The Four Horsemen, please tell Dot or another member of staff.*

'You'd better give me your phone number,' says Dot. 'I won't put it in the window, it's just so I can call you if anybody does know anything.'

'Sure, thank you.' I write it on a bit of paper and hand it

over. 'Right,' I say. I feel dejected now, and the lack of sleep is catching up on me. 'I guess we've taken up enough of your time. Thanks so much for everything. Please call me if you hear anything. Come on, Rosie . . .'

I start to turn towards the door and then I backtrack. I feel like I should buy something, to thank Dot for her help. There are some sets of earplugs on the counter, five pounds a pair. 'Actually, I could do with these,' I say, handing over the five shiny pound coins that were meant for Starbucks. They might be useful, I think, to drown out the noise of Mum's singing when she has her medieval music group round to the flat.

Dot smiles and wraps the ear plugs in a paper bag for me. 'Good luck,' she says. 'I promise I'll be in touch if I can help.'

'Fingers crossed,' I say, under my breath, as the door tinkles shut behind me.

I link arms with my friends and we head back onto Kentish Town Road, towards Camden High Street.

'She was lovely,' says Vix.

'Yeah.' I nod.

'And you never know, that poster might work.'

'Yeah.'

'You seem really quiet. You OK?'

'Yeah, I'm fine. I think I'm just starting to realise finding Dad's not going to be easy.'

'I know what you need,' says Rosie. 'Retail therapy. Come on . . .'

Unlike Rosie and Vix, I'm not a vintage clothes type of

girl, so we avoid the market and trawl around Camden's high-street stores, going first into All Saints, where I can't afford any of the clothes I like, and then into Gap and American Apparel. I buy some shiny, red leggings, not because I need them, but because they're bright and fun and just carrying them around cheers me up.

Vix and Rosie treat me to a coffee. It's a little too chilly to sit outside today, so we have our drinks inside Starbucks, where the walls are covered with a timeline of Camden history and pictures of all the famous people who've been born or lived here. The place is full of tourists with backpacks; we're probably the only locals in here. I often think how weird it is that thousands of people come to visit my neighbourhood every weekend.

'Have you spoken to Rich again, since last night?' Vix asks.

'No, not yet. I'm sure we will later.' I smile my fakest smile. 'It'll be fine.'

'Sure it will.'

'It was all a misunderstanding. My fault, really. I kept going on about my stupid nose. Anyway, we'll sort it out. We always do.'

I catch Vix giving Rosie a glance. It feels like they're ganging up on me.

'You're better than him, Sky,' Vix says. 'You don't need to be with someone who makes you feel bad about yourself.'

Now I feel defensive. 'He doesn't. Most of the time he's lovely.'

Vix shrugs. 'We just want you to be happy. And you don't seem it.'

'Yeah, well. It's not just Rich. Anyway,' I change the subject, 'how are things going with Laurie, Rosie?'

'Great,' says Rosie, a big grin lighting up her face. 'Really well. I might pop into the shop to see him later, on the way home. We're going out on a date tonight – cinema, I think.'

'Fantastic! So when are we going to get to meet him properly?'

'Soon, I promise. I just don't want to get too full on at the moment. You know, after Max.'

Max is Rosie's ex, and Rufus Justice's brother. He came to stay for the summer holidays and Rosie went out with him. But it didn't work out.

'Have you heard from Max since he went back to school?'

'We've chatted a couple of times online. But it's a bit weird. Vix is in touch with him though, aren't you, Vix?'

Vix nods. 'Yeah, we've been messaging a bit. He sounds happy. I think he has a new girlfriend too. He says he misses Camden though. He might come back for a week at Christmas.'

'Are you cool with that, Rosie?'

'Course,' she says. 'Why wouldn't I be? We'll be much better off as friends. That's what we always should have been.'

I don't say this aloud, but I can't imagine ever wanting to be friends with Rich, if we (and it's hard even to say this) split up. I just know that every time I saw him, I'd want to kiss him. It's weird: the more Rich is mean to me, or ignores me when he's with his mates, the more I want to be with him. I always think that it's only a matter of time before he looks at me and remembers how special we are together.

We chat about school stuff for a while, and gossip about what's been going on in our street lately. The Residents' Association has been plotting to get the art collective closed down and the police have been around a couple of times, banging on the door.

'There's something else I need your help with,' I say, eventually. I tell them about my visit to the doctor's surgery, earlier, and my embarrassing appointment with Rosie's mum.

Rosie is wide-eyed. 'I wondered why my mum asked how you both were before I came out. She was like, "How *are* Sky and Vix? It's so lovely that you're all such good friends." I thought it was a bit weird.'

'Ha! That's because she thinks I'm a loon. She says I need counselling.'

Rosie laughs. 'Seriously?'

I nod. 'Yeah. Next time I come round to yours, she'll probably have the men in white coats waiting for me.'

Vix doesn't seem to think it's funny. 'You're not mad, Sky, obviously, but she's right: you don't need a nose job.'

'Yeah, yeah. So you keep saying. Anyway, I'm going to find another doctor, one who can help. I've got a list of clinics from the back of a magazine.'

'Are you sure they're OK?'

'Course they are. *Vogue* wouldn't let just anyone advertise in the back, would they?'

'I guess not.' Vix seems unsure.

'So, I was wondering . . . I know it's a lot to ask on top of helping me find Dad, but will you both come with me? I'm a bit nervous about going on my own.'

'Course we will,' says Vix, without hesitating, and Rosie agrees. But they give each other another conspiratorial look. I pretend not to notice.

'After school, next week, would be good. I was thinking, if we all skip phys ed on Wednesday afternoon, it should give us plenty of time to see a few.'

We have another coffee, then walk back onto the High Street and say our goodbyes. Rosie's off to meet Laurie and Vix has to go to Sainsbury's to buy a few things for her mum. I'll probably go round to her house later tonight, to watch a DVD. On my way home, I take a detour past Dot's Music Shop. Dad smiles at me from the 'missing' poster in the window. I can't help wondering – or hoping, really – if soon he'll be smiling at me for real.

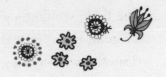

Chapter 11

Plastic
Fantasic

I'm lucky that Harley Street, where all the plastic surgery doctors seem to work, is very close to Camden Town, just on the other side of Regent's Park. If we had the time and the inclination, we could walk there. But today, we're getting the 27 bus from just behind Camden High Street instead. And hoping we don't bump into anyone from school or, even worse, our parents. I've got out of double netball by saying I had to go to the doctor (just not which sort). It was harder for Vix and Rosie because they're both in the same class at their school, which looks doubly suspicious. Rosie developed a 'migraine' and Vix said she had something important she had to do at home. Vix has never bunked off before, but everyone knows her mum is sick, so nobody doubted her. She feels guilty, which is making me feel guilty too, because she's only done it for me.

I was hoping my enthusiasm would be infectious, but I can tell that Rosie and Vix have been discussing my nose 'fixation' again and plotting about how they can talk me out of having surgery. I can tell by the sympathetic glances they keep giving me. Honestly, I think they only agreed to come with me because they're worried that someone might give me a nose job this afternoon, on the spot, and they want to make sure that doesn't happen. If only.

The afternoon isn't going well. So far, we've been to three of the clinics I found through the magazine listings, and I haven't got past the reception desks. It's always the same story.

'I'm here to see a doctor about my nose,' I tell the receptionist.

'Do you have an appointment?'

'No, I didn't know I needed one.'

'A referral letter?'

A what? 'Um, no, sorry.'

The receptionist eyes me suspiciously. 'How old are you, dear?'

'I'm nearly fifteen,' I say.

'I very much doubt any of our surgeons will operate on you at your age. And the doctor certainly won't agree to see you without a parent present, I'm afraid. I suggest you ask your mother to give us a call and make an appointment.'

'Look, we might as well go home,' says Vix, when we're outside on the street again. 'Like they all keep saying, you're too young for surgery. It's a waste of time.'

'They might not all say that. Someone might think I'm a special case.'

Vix sighs. 'OK. Where to next then?'

'Just up the road. Number 14B. The Metamorphosis Clinic.'

I like the name. It makes me think of caterpillars turning into beautiful butterflies, or ugly ducklings into swans. I'm dying for my chance to become a swan.

The Metamorphosis reception area is very plush, like a posh hotel, with huge leather sofas and an antique wooden table. Just being there makes me feel like I'm someone important. The table is covered with leaflets showing before and after pictures of smiling, satisfied patients. *Trust Metamorphosis for a perfect result*, they declare.

'Hello? Can I help you?' asks a heavily made-up woman with huge lips from behind the desk.

'Yes, I'm here to see someone about a rhinoplasty.' This time I call it by its proper name; I'm sure it makes me sound older and more serious. I've decided that if anyone asks my age again, I'll say I'm sixteen. If I'm going to have a nose job it doesn't matter if lying makes my nose grow a fraction (and I'm starting to doubt that it makes any difference); there'll just be a tiny bit more to shave off. By the time I have the actual operation, I'll have persuaded Mum to give her consent.

The receptionist pouts at me. It's probably the only expression she can manage. Her lips are so big that she can't close her mouth properly.

'The thing is, I don't have an appointment. Can somebody see me now?'

'Yes, you can have a preliminary consultation.' She stares at me for a moment and I think she's trying to work out if I'm old enough. 'Right. Well, the consultation fee is one hundred pounds. If you'd just like to fill in this form.' She hands over a questionnaire, attached to a clipboard.

A hundred pounds? I don't carry that kind of money around with me. I thought I wouldn't have to pay anything until I had the actual operation, which would have given me heaps of time to come up with a plan. 'Can I pay later?'

'No, I'm afraid you have to pay upfront. You can use a credit card if you like.'

Credit card? 'No, it's OK, I'll just go to the cashpoint. Is there one nearby?'

She directs me to a bank, five minutes' walk away.

'Did you see her lips?' Rosie says, taking my arm, as we march back up Harley Street. 'They were like two lilos stuck in the middle of her face!'

Vix giggles. 'Yeah, she's not a very good advertisement for the plastic surgeon. She couldn't move her eyebrows either.'

'Yeah, well,' I say. 'She had a nice nose, though, didn't she?'

'We're not actually going to the cashpoint, are we?' Vix asks. 'I mean, do you have a hundred quid?'

'Just about. Luckily my card is in my purse for emergencies.'

Out of the corner of my eye I see Vix and Rosie exchange one of their concerned glances. 'Are you sure about this?' asks Vix. 'It's a lot of money just to see a doctor when you don't —'

I don't let her say, 'don't need to'. 'I know. But it'll be worth it.'

We've reached the cashpoint. Anxiously, I put my cash card in the slot. I'm not meant to use it; the account has my birthday money and savings in it and Mum only got it for me in case of emergencies. (Which this *is*, kind of.) I think I've got about two hundred pounds left. But, if I'm careful with my allowance for the next few months, and do a bit of babysitting for the neighbours, I should be able to replace the money before Mum notices it's gone. It takes me a moment to remember my PIN but then I punch it in and the machine makes a whirring sound, before dispensing five crisp twenty-pound notes into the slot. 'Right,' I say, folding up the money and putting it into my purse. 'Let's go.'

'Listen, we really don't have to go back, Sky,' says Rosie. 'We could just walk through Regent's Park, have a coffee, or even an ice cream, and then go home.'

'No.' I'm determined. And nobody's been able to buy me off with an ice cream since I was about eight. 'You can go home if you like. I'm going to see the doctor.'

Rosie shrugs. 'OK, then, we're coming too. We're not letting you do it alone.'

We walk back to the clinic in silence. I hate knowing that my best friends aren't on my side; I've always thought they understood me completely. I hurts that they think I'm stupid or even crazy to want to have my nose fixed, and it makes me feel terribly alone.

I hand over my money and Big Lips passes me the questionnaire again. It asks me all kinds of questions about my health – most of which I can't answer – like whether I have any allergies, or if my relatives have heart problems. I fill in what I can, remembering to alter my birth date by two years.

Big Lips glances at the form and files it away in a tray. 'Right, Miss Smith. Take a seat. The doctor will be with you soon.'

Vix and Rosie sit down on either side of me. 'You promise you won't say a word when I see the doctor?' I say. 'Swear? You'll just sit there with me. Otherwise I'll go in on my own.'

Vix looks at Rosie. 'OK,' she agrees. Rosie nods.

There's nobody else in the waiting area, and so it isn't long before I'm ushered through to a consultation room. The doctor is sitting behind a large desk.

'Hello, I'm Dr Sierra,' he says, getting up to greet me. He's rather fat for a doctor and he hasn't shaved, but he looks jolly. He shakes my hand, a little too firmly. 'So what can I do for you, Miss Smith?'

'I'd like a rhinoplasty, please,' I say, brightly. It comes out a little too much like I'm ordering a burger at McDonald's.

'Ah, yes, of course.' He glances down at the questionnaire

I've filled in, then nods and peers at my nose. I flinch. He takes my face in his hands and gently moves it from left to right. I watch his eyes dart around as he studies my profile, then his brow furrows. I'm waiting for him to say, 'You don't need a nose job, your nose is perfectly OK,' like everybody else has, but he doesn't. Instead, he says, 'Yes, yes, I can see why you're concerned about the bend here, and the length. But don't worry. We can give you the perfect little nose.'

'Really? Seriously?'

'Oh yes, of course. I correct deformities like yours all the time. Take a seat, ladies, please. Half the celebrities you see on TV and in movies had a nose just like yours when they started out. You don't know it because they've had a subtle rhinoplasty.'

'Wow. I didn't realise.' I rack my brains, thinking of all the celebrities I know, wondering which of them was born with a nose like mine.

'So what were you thinking of? A Nicole Kidman, perhaps? That's very popular. Or a Kate Winslet? An Angelina, if you prefer?' He takes a folder out of his desk drawer and flips it open. Inside are pages and pages of pictures of beautiful women. He shows me a few, flicking through them so fast that I don't have time to see any of them properly. I didn't know I could pick my nose from a catalogue. To be honest, until this moment, I haven't even thought about what sort of nose I want, and certainly not whose. I've only been focusing on getting rid of mine. 'Yes, they all look great. What do you recommend?'

'Well, we could give you something a little like this.' He picks up a pad from his desk and scribbles something on it. It's a crude drawing of my face in profile. 'Now, if we shave off a little here to iron out the bump and reduce the tip slightly here, like so, we should end up with something like this.' He shows me the pad again. This time he's drawn an outline of my face with a smaller, straighter nose.

Rosie whispers something to Vix and giggles. I slap her leg.

Dr Sierra continues. 'The procedure will cost four thousand pounds. You'll have it at our affiliated private hospital in Highgate. Either I or one of my colleagues will perform it . . .'

He says something else, about black eyes and dressings and aftercare, but I can't take it in. All I can hear is a small voice in my head repeating 'Four thousand pounds. Four thousand pounds.' Where on earth am I going to find that kind of money? Have I got any rich relatives I don't know about? Is it possible that Mum once accidentally buried a stash under the floorboards and forgot about it? Maybe, if I ask for the next three years' allowance in advance and do lots of odd jobs for people, I might be able to manage it.

He's staring at me, hopefully. 'So we can arrange it all very quickly.'

'Uh, yes, I definitely want to go ahead. It's just, er, the money. I don't have it all right now.'

He smiles. 'That's not a problem. Sheila at the front desk

can give you some information about loans for plastic surgery. There are some very good rates around at the moment and we have excellent relationships with several finance companies.'

'Right . . .' I nod. I think he can't have read the form properly. It says I'm only sixteen; how the hell will I get a loan? Especially as I'm really only fourteen.

'So, if you want to sort out the finance side and then make another appointment, we can arrange a more in-depth consultation.' He glances at his watch. My time must be up. 'We look forward to hearing from you soon, Miss Smith,' he says, getting up from his chair and escorting me to the door. He holds out his hand again. 'Goodbye, my dear.'

Back outside, I can barely stand still with excitement. 'Wow! That was the most expensive twenty minutes of my life. Still, if I can somehow find the money, he'll do the op. He agrees I need it. That's cool, isn't it!'

Vix shakes her head. 'I still don't think you need it, hon.'

'He's a plastic surgeon and he knows about these things. If he thinks I do, then I do. He said I had a *deformity*.'

'Yeah, for four grand,' says Rosie. 'He'd probably have said your lips had a deformity and done them too, if you'd asked. I don't feel good about him. Are you sure he isn't dodgy? Maybe you should check him out on the internet.' God, she's sounding more and more like Vix every second. 'Don't you think he was a bit vague about everything except the money?'

'So? He has to earn a living. Your mum gets paid, doesn't she?'

'Yes, but it's not the same. She doesn't diagnose people with illnesses they don't have just so she can get some cash. Did you see that drawing he did? It was like something my little brother Charlie would draw. And he's seven.'

'It was only a sketch. Just to give me an idea.'

'Hmm,' says Rosie. 'Anyway, we can talk about this more later. Have you seen the time? It's almost five-thirty. We'd better motor or our parents will start wondering where we are.'

The 27 bus comes quickly and, within ten minutes, we're back in Camden. We say our goodbyes at the front door of my block of flats. 'It was nice of you both to come,' I tell them, as we hug. I try to sound genuinely grateful. 'Thanks.' Then I watch them walk up the street towards their houses. They walk very close together, apparently deep in conversation, and I'm sure they're conspiring about me again.

I loiter on the doorstep for a moment, not wanting to go inside. Maybe I should ring someone, I think. I dig my phone out from the bottom of my bag and remember that it's still switched off. While it comes back to life, I consider calling Rich to tell him that I've found a doctor to fix my nose, but change my mind almost straight away. He probably won't be sympathetic. He might not even pick up. Things have been worse than ever since our anniversary dinner. I can't think how to make them better.

Beep! There's a message on my voicemail, from a number I don't recognise. I'm half expecting it to be someone from school, telling me off for missing netball. I press play.

'Hello, Sky, it's Dot here. I thought you'd like to know that someone came in today and said they think they remember your dad. Please give me a call back.'

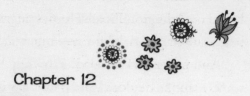

Chapter 12

Arlington House

I don't go inside my flat, after all. I turn around, walk back up my street and rush straight round to Dot's instead. She's shutting up the shop when I arrive, but she lets me in.

'Hello, Sky. You got my message then?'

'Yes, just now. Thanks so much for calling. Is this a bad time? I'm sorry, should I have phoned first?'

'It's not a problem. All right. A man came in earlier. He was walking past the window and saw the poster. He claims he knows your dad and said he'd be happy to meet you to tell you more.'

'That's amazing! I didn't expect anyone to get in touch so fast. What did he say?'

'His name is Reg. He lives in Arlington House, the homeless hostel on Arlington Road. He says he used to be a musician too, before he started drinking too much and taking drugs.'

'And he knows my dad? How?'

'He thinks he does.' She pauses, as if she isn't sure whether or not to tell me something. 'He says he knew him a few years ago.'

'Cool! When can I meet him?'

Dot smiles. 'Now, he seems nice and I'm sure he's perfectly trustworthy but we can't be certain he's genuine, and not just after a reward, or something. So I don't want you meeting him alone, especially if your mum doesn't know about it. It's definitely not a good idea for you to go to the hostel, either. I'm not sure how safe it would be for a young girl. So I'm going to get him to come back to the shop. You can meet him here with me, OK?'

'OK. Yes. Thank you. When?'

'When do you want?'

'How about right now?'

She laughs. 'I'm afraid I've got plans now. I'll give him a call if you like. How about after school tomorrow instead? If it's convenient with him.'

'OK, sure. Thank you again.'

I go to bed early but I don't sleep much and, when I do finally drift off I have strange dreams. In one of them, Dad is at Dot's music shop playing a guitar. He's dressed in a white doctor's coat, wielding a scalpel. Rosie and Vix are there too, and they're trying to stop him getting close to me. The morning can't come soon enough.

Just a day of school to get through and then maybe, maybe, maybe, I'll be one step closer to finding Dad. I've decided not to tell anybody I'm going to Dot's to meet Reg, not even my best friends. I feel it's something I have to do on my own this time, although I'm not sure why.

I arrive at Dot's just after four. She's busy in the shop, serving customers, so I loiter by the door, reading the leaflets in the display stand about all the music events in Camden. Eventually, she comes over to say hello.

'Reg said he'd be here at four-thirty. I tell you what: while we wait, you can help me sort out the sheet music, if you don't mind. It's all a bit of a mess.'

'Course,' I say, following her into the back office. It's good to have something to occupy me. I feel jittery and anxious. Every time I hear the sound of the door opening, I jump, wondering if it's Reg. I have no idea what he'll look like or what he's going to tell me. I keep looking at my watch. He's late. What if he doesn't come? Will I ever be able to find him?

'Don't worry,' says Dot. 'I'm sure he'll be here soon.'

At four-forty, I hear the peal of the door again and Dot goes out to the front. She pops her head back into the office. 'He's here,' she says, grinning. 'Come on.' Nervously, I follow her out. There's a man leaning on the counter. Almost bald, but for a few wisps of grey hair scraped across his forehead, he's wearing old jeans and a grubby jumper and carrying a beaten-up rucksack. I walk over to him, my pulse pounding. Dot hovers by the office door, and I'm not sure if she's out of earshot.

'Hello, my love,' he says, in an accent I can't place. Somewhere up north, a long time ago? How did he end up in Camden? He holds out his hand and I shake it, even though his fingernails are filthy. 'I'm Reg. You must be Sky, Connor's girl.'

Nobody's ever called me that before. *Connor's girl*. Hearing it feels strange. I nod. 'I'm trying to find him. To get to know him again. Dot says you might remember him.'

Reg peers at me closely and I try not to recoil. I can smell a faint, stale sweetness on his breath. He looks ancient, although he tells me he's only fifty-three. His face is craggy and lined and his sunken cheeks seem to drag down his eyes. I wonder what he used to look like, when he was young. He might have been handsome; it's hard to tell now.

'Yes, you're definitely Connor's daughter. Connor Carter. He was a good 'un. I believe our paths crossed about two or three years ago, when we were both in Arlington House.'

'My dad was homeless? That's awful!' I check myself. 'Oh God, I'm sorry, I don't mean to be rude. There's nothing wrong with it, I just mean . . . It was a shock . . .'

'Nobody ever wants to end up homeless,' he says, kindly. 'I used to have a wife and a family myself. Your dad was only there for a short while. I believe he got himself back on his feet again. Met a woman.' He winks at me. 'He was a bit of a charmer with the ladies, if I recall.'

'Oh.' I'm not sure what to say. I realise that, to my surprise, I feel angry. Far worse than knowing Dad was homeless and living in a hostel is knowing that he was living – literally – up the road and never contacted me. I might even have passed him on the street, queued up behind him in Sainsbury's, boarded the same bus.

I have to know. 'Did he ever mention me? His family? I have two sisters, you know.'

Reg concentrates hard. 'He sometimes talked about his girls but I can't remember what he said. Just that he was fond of you. He had some photos that he put above his bed. All pretty girls, his daughters. A couple of you just like him too.'

'He did?' This makes me feel slightly better. So Dad does love us after all. He hasn't forgotten that we exist. But I'm definitely the only one who looks anything like him. Isn't it strange what other people see?

'I told him about my kids too. All grown up now. Up in Manchester still, I suppose.'

He sounds sad and I'm not sure if I should ask about them. 'Oh, right. Sorry.'

'All water under the bridge now.'

'Was my dad OK? Was he well?'

'As well as can be expected. Bit of a drink problem, like most of us.'

I nod. 'You don't know where he went when he left, do you? An address? A number?'

Reg shakes his head. 'We weren't close,' he says, 'and when people move on they don't tend to stay in touch.'

'Oh.' I'm disappointed.

'But we did used to talk about his music – we even jammed together a couple of times. He told me about a couple of bands he'd played with – The Four Horsemen, and, er, The River Runners. They're quite well known on the circuit. I think they might still be gigging. Why don't you look them up?'

'Cool, thanks. The River Runners? Yes, I will do.' It's another lead. Probably just another dead end, but worth a try.

He pauses and I wonder what he's waiting for. Then I remember. God, this is awkward. 'Um, can I give you some money for, er, dinner or something, to say thank you?'

'You're very kind.' He looks down at the floor, embarrassed. 'Actually, what I'd really like are some strings. For my old acoustic.'

I glance at Dot, quizzically. She reaches over to a display unit on the counter and, without a word, passes me a set of strings, mouthing, 'We can sort it out later.' The label reads *Martin Light Gauge Strings*. I smile and hand them to Reg. He stuffs them into the back pocket of his jeans.

'See you around,' he says. 'Good luck finding your dad.'

'Thanks.' I smile. 'Take care of yourself.' I know it's mean but I hope I don't bump into him again. That would be too weird.

I don't go straight home after I say goodbye to Dot, although I should. Instead, I take a walk through Camden, noticing the things I usually try to avoid: the parts of Camden that the tourists don't come to see and that the expensive estate agents cover up in their glowing reviews. On the corner of the High Street, where it meets Camden Road, there's a group of drunks who meet up to hang around and swig from their bottles. The police move them on, but they're always back again a few days later. I wonder if my dad ever drank with these people. I pass the skinny woman who begs for money by pretending she needs cash for a Travelcard and, a few metres further on, the sweet, jolly man who tells you a joke in return for a pound, like a street stand-up comedian. Has my dad ever stopped people in the street and asked for cash?

At Britannia Junction, I cross the road and head up Parkway, turning into Arlington Road to see where Dad once lived. Arlington House has been refurbished recently, but it's been a men's homeless hostel for ever. It's on a leafy street, next to a row of very expensive Victorian Houses. That's the weird thing about Camden: wherever you look, you'll find rich people living right next door to the poorest. It's always been this way. Maybe that's why it attracts so many writers and musicians.

I stand outside for a while, hoping, wishing that Dad will emerge from the front door, so I can give him a hug and take him for a coffee. I know it's stupid. He doesn't live here any more and, anyway, I'm not eight; he probably wouldn't even recognise me. God, I might not recognise him. Then, when I start to feel chilly, I turn around and walk slowly home.

Chapter 13

On My Own

'I'm worried about you, Sky,' says Mum. 'Are you depressed?' She's come into my bedroom and sat down on my bed, uninvited. It's my own fault: I've been home for an hour and I haven't spoken to her at all. I came straight to my room, intending to start searching for The River Runners on the internet, but I felt sleepy and curled up on my bed instead.

'Sorry?'

'You're spending a lot of time on your own at the moment and when you are around you're really quiet. You're not eating much either. Is there something I can help with?'

Mum has always prided herself on how open her family is,

how we're all like friends, not like mother and daughters. She doesn't want us to have any secrets. That was easy when I was a kid, when the only secrets I had were knowing that my tooth was wobbly or that I'd taken the last slice of cake. Now I'm older, I don't want to be mates with my mum. It's not *normal*. There are some things I don't want her to know. And there are some things I just can't tell her.

I shrug. 'I'm fine, honestly.'

'You'd tell me if there was anything up, wouldn't you?'

'Course I would.' I grin my broadest grin. I hope she'll give up now and leave me in peace.

She doesn't. 'Is it Rich? I've noticed he hasn't been round lately.'

Rich. Now there's something I *really* don't want to talk about. I'm not even sure how I feel about it myself. Mum's right: he hasn't been around. I haven't been to his either, or hung out with him after school or at breaktimes. Since our horrible dinner night we've messaged a few times – short, cursory chats about school – but not much more. I'm sure he's avoiding me. I'm not even sure if he's my boyfriend any more.

'Everything's cool with Rich. We're both just busy with other stuff. Anyway, you're the one who was always saying it was getting too serious. So you should be glad I'm not seeing so much of him.'

'But I know you love him, Sky. And I don't want you to be unhappy. I remember what it feels like.'

I shrug again. 'Yeah, I know.'

She gets up and I hope she's decided to leave the room. Instead, she sits down right next to me and places her hands on my shoulders. 'How about a nice massage? Get those knots out. I'll go and fetch the essential oils from my room if you like.'

I shake her hands away. 'No thanks.'

She looks hurt. 'OK. If you won't talk to me, will you talk to Ocean?'

'I don't need to. Anyway, I've got Vix and Rosie.'

'Sometimes it's good to talk to someone who's a little older. Just to get a different perspective.'

'Ocean wouldn't understand. She's just like you. She's on your side.'

She flinches. 'I'm not on anyone's side.' Looking thoughtful for a moment, she goes on, 'Sky, is this is about your dad again?'

'Partly.' I don't want her to know that I've been actively looking for him. I certainly can't tell her about Reg. I wonder how she'd feel if she knew Dad had been homeless. She might even be glad.

'Actually, there is something you can help with.' I pause, for dramatic effect. 'I've found a doctor who'll give me a nose job.'

She seems genuinely shocked, which is exactly what I intended. 'What? When? Where?'

'Harley Street,' I tell her.

'You went to Harley Street and saw a plastic surgeon? How?'

'On the number 27 bus. It was easy.'

'This isn't something to joke about, Sky.'

'No, I know that. My nose is no laughing matter.'

She stares at my nose and sighs. 'Remember in India, those children we saw who had leprosy, the ones with cleft palates that hadn't been fixed? They had real disfigurements, Sky. They needed plastic surgery. You're just being vain.'

'Yeah, well, we don't live in India. We live in Camden Town. London. England. And I'm going to get my nose fixed. So if you really want to help me you can give me four grand to pay for it.'

She laughs – a strange, growly laugh. 'You know full well I don't have that sort of money. And, even if I did, I wouldn't give it to you so that you can deform your lovely face.'

'Fine. Then there's nothing you can help with, is there? So will you please just leave me alone now?' I know I sound mean. I can't help it. I guess I'm angry with her too.

She doesn't move. Maybe she's trying to think of something to say. Finally, she gets up and stands by the side of the bed, sadness in her eyes.

'I couldn't help noticing that you've taken your nose stud out,' she says, in a quiet voice. 'I thought it was just for school, but you never wear it at all any more.' She fingers her own stud, twisting it around so that catches the light from my bedside lamp. I shrug and she turns away.

'I never wanted it in the first place,' I say under my breath, as she leaves my room. 'It suits you much better.'

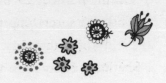

Chapter 14

The River Runners

The River Runners don't write any of their own music; they just do covers of old blues classics. And, despite searching for them on the web for the past hour, that is pretty much all I can tell you about them. There are a no pictures or profiles, and they don't have a Facebook page or even a MySpace account. I didn't think it was possible to be so invisible, not in the twenty-first century. Like The Four Horsemen, the only mentions I can find are in old listings pages, in announcements of evenings long since past and long since forgotten. Looking for Dad is beginning to feel like chasing after a wisp of smoke. Whenever I think I'm getting close, he vanishes again. It's almost as if he doesn't want to be found.

'Keep on going, Rosie,' I say, exasperated. We're at her house this time, using her computer. I've had a try, and so has Vix. Now it's her turn. 'There's got to be something else about them. There's just got to be.'

She groans. 'I'm doing my best here, Sky. There's just pages and pages of gigs. They don't say anything useful.'

'I know! There's never details of the line up, no reviews and no contact emails! How the hell do they get booked? Or paid?'

Rosie sighs. 'There must be a booker or an agent or something. All I can see are things like, *July fifteen, eight p.m., support: The River Runners, Blues classics with an Irish twist,* whatever that means.'

'It's the type of stuff Dad used to play on his CDs when I was a kid,' I explain. 'Eric Clapton and people like that, I think. Which is hopeful, because I'm sure it must be the right band, at least. We just don't know if Dad's with them any more. Or how to contact them to ask.'

'What about looking at the results in date order?' Vix suggests. 'Like clicking *results from the past year* or even just the past month. That way you'll cut out a lot of the really out of date stuff.'

'Genius idea, Vix. Go on, Rosie.'

'OK. Let's try it . . .'

Rosie presses return and a new list of webpages fills the screen. 'That's better. There's only a few results now. It's a little more manageable.'

'So?' I ask. 'Is there anything really up to date?'

'Yeah, there's a couple from this year! So at least we know they're still going.'

'That's a relief. And?'

'Ah, they played some pub in Reading about a month ago.'

'Whereabouts is Reading again?'

'I dunno,' says Rosie. 'I think it's somewhere near London.'

Vix giggles. 'Have you actually ever left Camden, Rosie?'

'Ha ha. Not if I can help it. Why would I?' She pauses. 'Hang on . . .' Her voice goes up a whole octave. 'Oh my God! Sky! You're not going to believe this . . .'

'What?'

'I think I've found something amazing. Yeah! I have! The River Runners are playing a gig next Saturday night. And you're going to die when you hear where it is!'

'Stop teasing me, please. Just tell me . . .'

'It's the Dublin Castle. In Camden!'

'Seriously? Are you sure? The pub on Parkway?'

'Yeah, I've double checked. They're on the bill. This coming Saturday.'

'Let me see . . .' I usher her off her chair and take her place, scrolling down the screen three times, just to make sure. She's right. The River Runners are due to play in Camden in a few days' time. I'm so excited I feel hot and shaky. 'Oh my God, what are the chances? What if we hadn't done this search now? If we'd waited a few days we might have missed them. It must be fate. We've got to go!'

'Absolutely. There's just one problem,' says Vix. 'It's Carrie's fifteenth birthday party on Saturday night. We said we'd all be there. And you were going to try to sort stuff out with Rich there too, remember?'

Of course I remember. I've already chosen my outfit and practised my make-up to ensure I look the best I possibly can look. I've even rehearsed what I'm going to say to Rich. The plan is to show him that I am lots of fun, just like I used to be. I'm going to dance with him and kiss him and make him fall back in love with me. 'OK, what time's the gig?' I scroll back up the page. 'It's says here that doors open at eight-thirty. There's a few bands playing. I don't know when The River Runners will be on, so we'll have to get there for the start.'

'Maybe we can do both,' says Vix. 'Go to the gig and then the party.'

'Maybe.' Suddenly, making things better with Rich doesn't seem so important – not when I am about to meet my dad. 'Rich can wait. One night won't make a difference, will it? Whatever happens, I'm going to see my dad. And I'm not sure that once that's happened I'll want to go to a party. He'll probably want to buy me dinner or something, start getting to know me properly again.'

'Don't get ahead of yourself,' Vix cautions. 'You don't even know if he's still in the band. Or, even if he is, how he'll be when he sees you. He might not . . . Look, don't get too excited yet, OK?'

'I can't help it. This is the best chance I've ever had of

seeing him again. There must be a reason why he keeps coming back to Camden. Don't you think?'

Vix hugs me. 'Let's just play it by ear,' she says. 'The good thing is that because of the party we already have an excuse to get dressed up and go out on Saturday night. Nobody will ask any questions.'

'That's true. I can't wait. It's going to be a big night!'

Chapter 15

D-Day

Camden on a Saturday night is crazy, even crazier than usual. It's busier than most town centres are during the day, with so many people pouring out of the tube and into the bars, restaurants and pubs that you can barely walk up the High Street. There are tourists still drifting around hours after the markets have closed, gig-goers arriving from all over London, locals out for a Saturday-night drink or cinema visit, and gangs of kids hanging around outside the kebab shops, some of them spoiling for a fight. The pavements are littered with Coke cans and cigarette butts and fast-food wrappers, and there's so much music playing in so many different venues that you can feel the vibration from all the bass drums through the soles of your shoes.

I'm not really supposed to go out in Camden on a Saturday night, not even with Rosie and Vix. The later it gets, and the drunker people become, the more edgy it feels. I know that there have been a few stabbings and that people have been mugged, but that can happen anywhere. I'm not scared – Camden is very well lit and I'm streetwise. And tonight, not even a riot would stop me going out. Because tonight is the night that I'm going to find my dad. Finally.

'Don't get your hopes up too much,' says Vix, as we all get ready at her house. 'We might not get in.'

But I'm not listening. I've never felt so sure of anything: Dad is going to be there. I can sense it, I can picture it, I know it. Mum's always told me to follow my instincts, she even said I was a bit psychic once, although I laughed at her for that. Tonight, I think she might be right. My gut is telling me it's going to happen. It's telling me so strongly that I haven't been able to eat a thing all day. I've never felt so nervous, not before a first date, or even an exam.

'Look up for me and don't blink,' I say, changing the subject and trying to distract myself. I'm helping Vix with her make-up because she looks the youngest. I think you have to be at least sixteen to get into the Dublin Castle for a gig, which is easy for me, and not too difficult for Rosie either. I can't help noticing how pretty Vix looks with eyeliner; she really should make more of her eyes. She's still a bit of a tomboy but, I have to say, when she makes an effort she's actually the prettiest of all of us. She just doesn't know it.

I hand her the mirror. 'I think you're done.'

Vix peers at her reflection and smiles. 'Thanks, hon.'

'Maybe there'll be someone cute at the party for you,' says Rosie. 'Or even the gig. You never know. We all look super hot, if I say so myself.'

Vix shrugs. 'Doubt it. And you've got Laurie, remember. Anyway, it's Sky's night. We're not looking for cute guys, we're looking for one dad-shaped guy.'

The thought sends butterflies rushing through my stomach again. I look at my watch. 'I guess we should go. Do I look OK?'

It's been hard choosing what to wear. I need to look like I'm going to a friend's house party and, at the same time, old enough to get into a gig, pretty enough for Rich (in case I do make it to the party later) and, most important of all, at least a little like the daughter Dad remembers. I've settled on a stretchy, black and white stripy dress, which I can cover with a little black cardigan. I think it works.

'You look gorgeous, Sky,' says Rosie. I can tell she's checking out my make-up and that she wants to say something about the excess bronzer on my nose. I stare her out, and she doesn't.

We're too early to go to the gig but, as far as our parents our concerned, we're going to a party just up the road, and they agreed that if we went early enough we could walk there together. So we're planning to detour around the block and then cut across Camden Street and back onto Camden Road, before crossing Britannia Junction and heading up Parkway. We'll hang out in a café until it's time. Our parents never go into Camden on a Saturday night, so nobody will spot us.

We walk briskly, arm in arm, saying very little. I'm lost in my own thoughts, imagining the moment when Dad's eyes meet mine. Will he be pleased to see me? What will he say? And what if he isn't happy? What if he's angry or, worse, what if he blanks me? I don't think I could handle that. Tonight the emos are queuing at the entrance to the Underworld as we pass, waiting to see some band or other. Part of me wishes I was like them, a member of a group, sure of where I belonged. Life would be so much simpler, so much easier if I fitted somewhere. But I don't want to be a clone, I want to be me. Whoever she is. I grip my friends' arms tighter. Thank God they're with me; I know I couldn't do this alone.

We while away an hour sitting in The Goodfare, an Italian café on Parkway that's painted bright red and green and which we've all been coming to with our families since we were kids. Rosie and Vix order big bowls of pasta, and try to feed me forkfuls, complete with 'mmm' and 'ahh' noises to tempt me, but I wave them away. I'm still not hungry. 'I'll get a bag of crisps later,' I tell them.

We're virtually the first to arrive at the Dublin Castle for the gig, although the pub is already filling up. There's nobody on the door but, to make ourselves less conspicuous, we go in on the coat tails of a group of friends. Nobody spots us.

Ignoring the bar, we head straight into the back room, where the bands play. Someone is sound checking, a group of young guys, definitely not Dad's band. There are a few different acts on the bill tonight, supporting the main band. From the look of the flyer, I think The River Runners are on second. We stand at the back of the room, letting the crowd file in in front of us.

The first band is rubbish, all screechy guitars and out-of-tune singing, and they seem to go on for hours. I will them to finish, growing ever more jittery. I'm feeling lightheaded and wobbly, although that might just be because I haven't had any dinner. When, at last, they're done, the lights come back on and practically everyone else goes to the bar. We crouch down on the dirty, sticky floor, using our jackets as cushions. Rosie tries to calm my nerves by telling me a story about Laurie's boss, but I'm not listening. 'I'm going to the loo,' I say. My bladder must be empty – I went twice in The Goodfare – but I can't stop feeling like I need to pee. Anyway, it should kill a few minutes.

There's a long queue for the Ladies and, by the time I return, the room has begun filling up again. Finally, the lights dim and my stomach lurches horribly. A band is coming onstage, but I can't see properly – there are too many people in front of me: someone with a backpack, someone else with a hat, someone too tall.

'Come on,' I shout, grasping my friends' arms and dragging them towards the stage, through any gap I can find.

Someone jostles me with their elbow, someone else steps on my foot, but I don't feel it. I just keep going forward. I need to be close enough to the stage to see clearly, but not too close. Just close enough.

'Hello, Camden,' says the lead singer, as the spotlight hits him. 'We're The River Runners. And it's great to be back here at the Dublin Castle!'

There's a crash of drums and the wail of a guitar. The crowd cheers. The music must be deafeningly loud, although I can barely hear it. I'm in my own little bubble. I scan the stage, glancing from one musician to the next, as they step out of the shadows and into the glare of the stage lights. And suddenly, he's there in front of me, a harmonica pressed to his lips.

Dad. MY DAD.

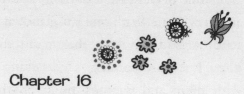

Chapter 16

Meeting Dad

With a clash of cymbals, The River Runners finish their set. We hang back as they pack up their gear, then watch as they come offstage and head to the bar. Vix, Rosie and I follow close behind, keeping them in our sights, trying not to get lost in the surge of people vying for a drink. We stand still for a few minutes, not speaking. I'm nervous as hell and have no idea what I'm going to say to Dad. All I know is I can't let him leave before we've spoken.

'I think I need to do this on my own,' I say. 'Do you two mind waiting for me?'

Vix nods. 'Sure you do. No problem.' She lets go of my hand and mouths, 'Good luck.'

I smile bravely, but I don't feel brave. I feel tiny and naked and very alone. With one last glance at my friends, I walk over towards Dad, my legs shaky and difficult to control. He doesn't see me coming. He's talking to someone, laughing with them and slapping them on the back. I notice how much fatter he is, how much older he looks. Shorter, too, although that could just be because I've grown so much. There's a pint glass in his hand. Half empty.

It's my dad. It's my dad. It's my dad. Those words keep running through my mind, blocking out all other thoughts. It's been a long time since I was eight years old, but part of me still wants to run up to him and hug him, and let him spin me around until I'm so dizzy that when he puts me down I have to cling on to his legs for support.

But I don't. Of course I don't. I walk up to him, stand beside him, wait for him to finish speaking and then tap him gently on the shoulder. 'Dad?' I say. It comes out like a question. I don't know why.

He doesn't seem shocked to see me. There's a flicker of something in his eyes – surprise, recognition, fear, annoyance, I can't tell – but it's gone in an instant. It's almost as if he's been expecting me to pitch up at one of his gigs, one day. Or maybe he's just good at hiding his emotions.

'Sky-blue?' he says. 'Well, well, well. How the devil are you?' He hugs me, but it's not a Dad hug. It's a hug you'd give an old friend. 'I didn't think I'd be seeing you tonight, so I didn't.'

'I tracked you down,' I tell him. 'On the internet.'

'You always were a clever girl,' he says. 'I'm not so easy to find.'

'No, you're not. I . . . we still live in Camden. Just up the road. I can't believe you're playing here tonight and...' I want to say, 'and didn't tell me,' but I'm scared it'll anger him, or make him run away. '. . . and here you are.'

'Camden Town's a good place for gigging.'

'Yes it is.' I don't know what else to say. I've had six years to think of something and now I can't find a single word. I want to cry, laugh, shout, kiss him and hit him, all at the same time. I want to know where he's been for the past six years, to ask him why he didn't keep in touch, to tell him about my life. But I can't do any of that. It's not the time, or the place. We're in a busy, noisy pub, surrounded by strangers, with his band mates and friends only inches away. A young woman with dark hair is standing next to him, talking to the drummer. I noticed her during the gig, at the side of the stage, singing along with the band. She keeps staring at me. She must be Dad's girlfriend, even though she doesn't look much older than me. I hate her on sight, just for that.

'Would you like a drink?' he asks.

'Um, yes. A diet coke, please.'

'Nothing stronger?'

'I'm only fourteen, remember,' I say quietly.

He peers at me, and it looks as if he's doing calculations in his head. 'Yes, I suppose you are. You all grow up so fast, nowadays, it's hard to keep track.'

That niggles. I look over at Rosie and Vix, who are standing by the wall. Rosie waves. They seem awkward, like they don't really want to be here. I'm not sure I want them to be here either, even though I don't want them to leave yet.

'So what have you been up to?' says Dad, handing me my drink, and steering me over into a corner, away from his party. 'Are you still at school?'

What age does he think people leave school in Camden? 'Yes, just started doing my GCSEs.'

'Ah. And do you like it?'

'It's OK, I guess.'

This is far more awkward than I was expecting. We shouldn't be making small talk. He's my dad.

'I see. So how are your sisters?'

'They're good, thanks.'

'And your ma?'

'She's OK.' I pause. 'She doesn't know I'm here, in case you're worried.'

'I see,' he says. 'I daresay I'm not her favourite person.'

I shrug. This isn't a conversation I want to get into. What can I say? *My mum hates your guts and wishes she'd never met you, and she warned me not to try to find you.* Instead, I say, 'I like your band. You're really good.'

'Aye, we're all right. The boys and I go way back. I play in a couple of other bands too. I've done a bit of session work here and there. So do you play anything, Sky?'

'Not really. I'd like to learn the guitar.'

'It's a fine instrument.'

'Yes.' *Maybe he could* . . . No, I can't ask that. We stand in silence for a moment. 'I've really missed you, Dad.' I don't mean to say it, the words just pop out.

He seems embarrassed, taken aback. 'Well, of course I've missed you too. But —'

'Sky?' Rosie has materialised at my side. That girl has the worst timing. 'Sorry to interrupt but we should go to the party, if we're going to go,' she says. 'As long as you're OK.'

'Sure.' I'm aware I sound hesitant. 'Dad, this is my friend, Rosie. Rosie, this is my dad.'

He shakes her hand. 'Delighted to meet you,' he says.

She smiles. They've met before, a long time ago, but maybe neither of them remembers. 'I enjoyed your set. Do you ever play any festivals? I've got a friend who's in a band, Rufus Justice from Fieldstar. You might have met him . . .'

'Aye, I've heard of them, but we're not really on the same circuit.'

Vix appears from the direction of the toilets. She seems shy of Dad, a bit wary, maybe.

'Hi,' she says, quietly. I introduce them and Dad shakes her hand too.

'So you girls all have a party to go to?' he says. 'That's great.' It feels like he's trying to get rid of me, or maybe I'm just being paranoid.

'Oh no, I'm not going yet,' I say, appealing to Dad with my

eyes. We haven't talked yet, not properly. And if I go now, I might never see him again.

'We'll stay if you want us to,' says Vix.

'No, no, it's OK, you should go,' I say. 'Anyway, you've got to be there when Rosie's dad arrives to pick you up.'

'Will you come along too, later?'

'I dunno. I don't think so. I'll be all right, whatever. Just make up an excuse for me. And tell Rich I'll call him tomorrow.'

'OK, then . . .' Rosie is putting her jacket on, but Vix seems hesitant. 'I'm worried about how you'll get home.'

I glance at Dad again. 'You'll see me home, won't you?'

He nods. 'Aye. I'll see you right.'

'Promise you'll call us if you need us,' says Vix. 'And text us to let us know you're home safely.'

'Course I will. No worries.'

I watch them leave and then turn back to Dad. We grin at each other, awkwardly, and I'm suddenly aware that I'm now alone, in a pub, at ten p.m. on a Saturday night, with a man who's almost a stranger and who quite possibly doesn't really want me to be here. Not to mention that if my mum finds out, I'll be grounded till I'm twenty-five. I could be with Vix and Rosie at a friend's party, making up with my boyfriend. Am I crazy?

'Come and sit down,' Dad says, motioning to a table where his bandmates are now sitting. 'I'll introduce you to my friends.'

I look for the dark-haired woman, so I can ask if she's Dad's girlfriend, but she seems to have left already.

'This is Sky,' says Dad, as we approach the table. 'Sky, this is John, Mike and Shane, and Mike's girlfriend, Sarah.'

I smile at them, shyly, and Sarah moves her chair a little so that I can sit down.

'Nice to meet you, Sky. So how do you know Connor?' she asks.

'He's, um, er . . .' Am I allowed to say it?

Dad chuckles. 'She's one of my long lost daughters, come to find me. Tracked me down on the internet, she did.' He makes it sound like a joke.

That niggles too. *I'm not lost*, I think. *I've been here all the time. You're the one who got lost.*

'Ah, right, then.' Sarah doesn't seem surprised. Perhaps long-lost daughters track their fathers down and turn up at gigs every day in her world. 'And where do you live?'

'I live here, in Camden, just down the road.'

'Marvellous! That's a stroke of luck.'

'I know.'

'Pretty girl,' says Shane, who's been studying me. 'You look a lot like your dad, don't you?'

I'm embarrassed. Now they'll all be staring at my nose. 'So people say.'

'Aye, I guess she does,' says Dad. 'There's no doubt you're a Carter, my girl.' He sounds proud, as if he's done his dad job just by passing on his genes.

Mike gets up to buy another round. We all sit and chat about gigs and travelling and people they've met along the way. Dad treats me like one of his mates, including me in the conversation, telling me jokes that make me blush. I have a good time but it feels stilted, slightly surreal. And I don't get a chance to talk to him the way I want to. Not alone, or about anything important. Maybe tonight just isn't the right time.

I check my watch. It's almost eleven-thirty. Vix and Rosie will be leaving the party, and I have to arrive home around the same time as them, so that nobody suspects anything.

'I really need to leave now, Dad.' I search his eyes for a trace of disappointment. If it's there, I can't see it.

'Aye, it's late,' he says, taking my wrist and studying my watch. I notice that he doesn't wear one. I can't remember if he used to. 'Now, will you be OK getting back?'

I nod and give him an expectant look, but he doesn't offer to walk me home, even though he promised Vix he'd look after me. 'Um, it's kind of late,' I point out. 'Would you mind coming with me?'

'Aye,' he says. 'I'll walk you back, so I will.'

I get up from my chair. My legs are stiff. I've been sitting, tensely, in one position for too long. Dad gets up too. I notice that he's not as sprightly as he used to be. His knees creak and he holds his back with his hand. I think: you wouldn't be able to pick me up and spin me round any more, even if you wanted to.

He has a quick word with some of his friends, and then we

leave the Dublin Castle and set off down Parkway together. We don't talk much; he seems to be in a hurry and we have to keep skirting around the drunk people spilling out of pubs, or queuing up for kebabs by the tube station.

Once we're on Camden Road, just past Sainsbury's, he stops, suddenly. 'You'll be all right from here, won't you? You're only a few minutes from home now.'

Maybe he's afraid of bumping into Mum, I think. 'Um, sure,' I say. I've never walked home alone through Camden Town, this late. I'll be OK, I tell myself. Walk fast, keep your head up, don't make eye contact with anyone, don't stop.

He leans over to hug me goodbye. This time I'm aware that his breath smells of stale beer and cigarettes.

'Good to see you, girl,' he says.

'You too, Dad.' I hesitate. If I wait for an invitation, it might never come. 'Will I see you again?'

'We're playing again in Camden in a couple of weeks. The Blues Kitchen. Come along,' he says. 'Bring those lovely friends of yours.'

That isn't exactly the answer I was hoping for. 'OK. Um, can I have your number?' It feels weird asking my own dad for his contact details. But he hasn't offered them and I'm scared that if I don't ask for them, I might lose contact with him again for good.

He looks pained. 'OK,' he says, 'but I don't want your mother to have them.'

'Course not. Like I said, she doesn't know I'm here.'

He takes a scrap of paper out of his pocket, and scribbles his number on it with a chewed-up biro. His handwriting is slanted, just like mine. I slide it into the inside pocket of my bag, zipping it tightly to make sure it doesn't fall out. He doesn't ask me for my number.

'Bye, then, Dad,' I say. I hug him again and take a deep breath, steeling myself for my walk alone up Camden Road, towards my street. As I take my first steps, I turn around to see if he's watching me, keeping me in his sights until he knows I'm safe. But all I can see is his back disappearing into the Saturday night crowds.

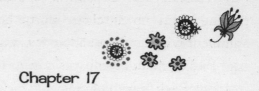

Chapter 17

Revelations

I'm home safe. I have so much 2 tell u, I text Rosie and Vix, the minute I climb into bed. I'm expecting to hear instant beeps in reply, because I know they'll both be dying to hear about what happened with Dad, but there's only silence. Ten minutes pass. Still silence. How maddening – I really want to talk to them. I want to tell them about Dad and his friends, and having to walk back part of the way alone, and crossing the street to avoid a drunk guy, and how I managed to get away without talking to Mum because she was doing a meditation session with crystals in the living room when I came in. I look at my alarm clock. It's quarter past midnight; surely they won't be asleep yet? Maybe they're still at the party. No. They can't be. I know for a fact that Rosie's dad was picking them up at eleven-thirty because Rosie had an argument with her mum about it being embarrassingly early. And Rosie's mum *never* backs down.

I call Rich next but he's not picking up, which is less surprising, given the way things have been lately. Is he annoyed that I didn't show up at the party? Was he hoping we'd patch things up too? I hope I haven't messed up my chances. I did text him to let him know that I was meeting my dad, and I half thought he might be interested enough to ask me about it. But no. He just texted back to say, *That's cool, have fun,* and nothing more.

I try to read while I'm waiting for someone to contact me, to take my mind off everything, but I'm far too hyper to concentrate. So I call Rosie and Vix, with no success. Then I attempt to sleep, but my eyes won't stay shut and my heart is going *boom, boom, boom* in my chest. Instead, I lie flat on my back, staring up into the dark ceiling, going over and over the night in my mind. And, somehow, at some time, I must fall asleep, because when I next turn over to look at my clock it's ten a.m. and the sun is glaring through the cracks at the sides of my blind.

My phone remains strangely free of text messages from Rosie or Vix. They're probably not awake yet, I tell myself. But, by midday, when I still haven't managed to reach them, I begin to worry. I don't have any evidence, but now it feels like they're avoiding me. I can't remember them ever ignoring a message before. Maybe they're just bored of the whole Dad thing. They have gone out of their way to help me up until now. Have they had enough? I call Rosie, and then Vix, again. Both phones go straight to voicemail. I don't leave a message.

When I come out of the shower there is, at last, a brief text message from Rosie, but all it says is: *Glad u got home safe. Will call 18r x.* Strange. Usually, she and Vix would be texting me frantically to find out exactly what they've missed. I text to say I'm up for a chat now, but don't hear anything back. So I get dressed and kill some time looking at clothes on a website I like, clicking back and forth with no intention of buying anything. By now it's after one and I'm starting to drive myself crazy with my paranoia. I call my friends one more time. Rosie's phone is still going to message, but Vix's rings. And rings. And rings. At last, when I'm certain the call is going to go to voicemail again, she picks up.

'Vix! I've been trying you for ages!'

'Oh hi, Sky,' she says, her voice flat. 'Sorry, I just woke up.' But she doesn't sound half asleep. She sounds weird.

'Oh right. Are you and Rosie OK? Was the party good?'

'I'm fine. Rosie's fine. I spoke to her earlier.'

Earlier? I thought she'd literally just woken up. Vix really is a hopeless liar. So my friends have been talking to each other? But not to me. About me, then? Something is definitely going on.

'Has something happened, Vix? Why didn't you reply to

my texts? Are you upset with me?'

'No, course not.' Her voice sounds shaky and nervous. 'I didn't get the ones from last night until I woke up. So how was your dad? Do you like him? Did you go on somewhere else with him?'

I realise that all my excitement about meeting Dad has dissipated. 'I'll tell you about Dad later. But I *know* there's something you aren't telling me. Your voice sounds weird. I'm getting really worried now!'

She pauses. 'OK. There is something ... I don't want to talk about it over the phone, though. I'm coming round now. OK?'

'OK ...'

She hangs up. I'm feeling really freaked out now. What has she got to tell me that she can't tell me over the phone? We're supposed to be meeting later, anyway. What can't wait till then?

It only takes a few minutes to walk from Vix's house to my flat but today it seems an eternity. I pace my bedroom while I wait, a sick, sinking feeling in my stomach. It's like queuing in line for an exam when you haven't done any revision and know you're going to fail. It's clear that whatever she's going to tell me can't be good news.

When the doorbell rings, I sweep across the hall to the intercom, buzzing Vix in, without checking that it's her. I grab her at the top of the stairs. 'What is it Vix? Please tell me. Has something happened? Have I done something to upset you and Rosie? Are you annoyed with me?'

'No, no. Nothing like that.' She motions to my bedroom, and I nod, leading her inside. When the door is shut she beckons me to sit down beside her on the bed, and takes a deep breath. 'It's Rich,' she says.

'Rich? Is he OK? Is he hurt? I tried to call him earlier too, but his phone was switched off. Has he had an accident?'

'No, no, nothing like that either. I don't even know how to say this. Oh God. Um.' She swallows hard. 'OK, I'm just going to come out with it. Rich snogged someone else at the party last night. I'm really sorry, hon. I know it must be a big shock.'

I let out a huge snort of a giggle. I don't know why; nothing is funny. Quite the opposite. But the giggle bursts out of me spontaneously, like a hiccough. Sometimes, when something really bad happens, like now, I laugh. It happened when Mum told me my grandma had died. It's totally inappropriate and really quite embarrassing, but it's also completely beyond my control.

Vix doesn't know how to handle it. There I am, laughing hysterically, when she expected me to burst into tears, or be angry, or disbelieving. She puts her arms around my back and hugs me until I stop laughing. Then I start to sob. She hugs me harder.

I feel totally numb now. 'Who was it? I need to know.'

'Just some girl,' says Vix, softly. 'You don't know her. It doesn't really matter who it was.'

'It does to me. Just tell me. Please.'

Vix takes a deep breath. I don't know why she's so reticent; I'm going to find out anyway. I'm sure the news will have spread round school by Monday morning. Oh God, I'm going to have to face Rich in school. 'It's not a friend, if that's what you're worried about.'

I suppose that's something. I couldn't bear the double betrayal. 'Someone from my class at school?'

'No, she goes to my school,' says Vix. 'She's nobody, really. I'm not even sure you've met her. It's not important. The fact is, Rich is a cheating skank and you're better off without him.'

'I need to know her name. I don't know why. I just need to be able to picture her.'

Vix shrugs. 'It was Donna. Donna Rice.'

'OK, thanks.' What a stupid thing to say. It's not OK. It's far from OK. Now I know exactly why Vix didn't want to tell me. Not because of who Donna is, or because of anything she's done. (I've only met her a couple of times, and she seemed all right. Quite sweet, really.) It's because she is physically the opposite of me. She's blonde and short and cute and, worst of all, she has the tiniest little snub nose. A nose that won't get in the way of kissing. An image of Rich and Donna snogging passionately, just like he used to do with me, seeps into my mind and, no matter how hard I try, I can't push it away.

'Are you all right, Sky? You've gone very quiet.'

'I'm fine,' I tell her. But my voice falters, so it's clear that I'm not.

'You're much prettier than her. And so much nicer, and more intelligent, and funnier too. Rich is an idiot.'

'How can you say I'm prettier?'

'Because it's true. Her nose is like a pig's snout. Her whole face is mushy and flat. I wouldn't want to look like her in a million years.'

She's lying. 'I would,' I say. 'I'd kill to look like her.'

Now I know. I was never Rich's type. He's just like all the other boys. Nobody wants a girl with 'character' or 'interesting' features. They want blonde, cute, sweet-looking cliché girls. Everything he said was a lie. I was always second best, a consolation prize. As soon as he had the opportunity to get off with a girl who was more his type, he took it. Maybe I shouldn't just fix my nose. Maybe I should sort out my hair too, grow it longer, get some highlights done, buy some new make-up.

'It'll be all right, Sky, I promise. I know you're upset now but you'll be so much better off without him. I'll go and get Rosie and we can do something together this afternoon, to cheer you up.' She hugs me again. 'Go to the market if you like, or out for tea, or just stay in and watch a film. Whatever you like.'

I'm not listening. I'm too distracted. 'I need to talk to Rich.'

She sighs. 'Is that a good idea, hon?'

'I don't know,' I tell her, 'but I've got to do it.'

'Want me to stay while you do it?'

'I think I want to be on my own.'

'OK,' she says, giving me one last hug and getting up from my bed. 'Call me later. Promise?'

I nod. 'I promise.'

I wait until I hear the front door shut and then I start to cry again. What should have been one of the best weekends of my life is turning out to be the worst.

I decide not to call Rich, after all. I'm not sure what to say and I don't want him to guess that I've been crying or, even worse, to make me blub down the phone to him. Anyway, he probably wouldn't pick up. I text instead.

I know, is all I say.

He doesn't respond immediately. I lie on my bed staring at my phone, willing it to beep. Surely, after six months together, he's not going to pretend I don't exist.

Sorry, he texts back. Nothing else. Is that it?

I think u owe me more than that. Can I come round 2 c u?

Another few minutes. Is it such a hard question to answer? Or is he enjoying torturing me?

Finally . . . *Bad idea.*

I knew he wouldn't want to see me. I'm annoyed but, to my surprise, it also comes as a relief. *Can we talk online?*

OK. I'll message u.

Yeah, right. It'll be next Christmas, if I know Rich. *Now. OK?*

Another pause. *OK.*

I leap off my bed and propel myself over to my computer,

logging into my instant messaging service as quickly as I can, so he can't make some excuse about not finding me and giving up. It takes a moment for his name to appear. *RichieB01*. I've seen it on my screen so often over the past six months. I wonder if I ever will again.

Hello, I type.

RichieB01: *Hi. How r u?*

Like he cares. I'm not going to waste time making small talk or making him feel better.

Me: *How could you do that to me?*

RichieB01: *Here we go. Look, Sky, I'm sorry u found out like that. I didn't plan it. But it's not like we were together any more.*

Me: *What?!!!! Are you serious????!!!!*

RichieB01: *We were over.*

Me: *No we weren't. We haven't split up. I think I might remember if we had.*

RichieB01: *Yeah, well, maybe I didn't actually say you're dumped, but after that night in the restaurant . . . well, I kind of thought you realised it was finished.*

Me: *No, I didn't. I kept trying to sort it out. Remember?*

RichieB01: *No. Anyway, now you know.*

Me: *You don't have to be so mean. I thought you loved me.*

I'm aware I sound all clingy and pathetic and girly, exactly what he hates most, but I can't help it.

RichieB01: *Get over it, Sky. We're too young to be serious. And it hasn't been fun for ages.*

Me: *So u never loved me?*

RichieB01: *I dunno. Maybe. Anyway, we're better as friends.*

I don't want to be his friend. I want to be his girlfriend.

Me: *I guess.*

RichieB01: *So we're cool then?*

Me: *Yeah.*

I've never felt less cool in my life. So, I might as well ask him . . . I mean, I've got nothing to lose, have I?

Me: *Why did you have to pick Donna, of all people?*

RichieB01: *What do you mean?*

Me: *Why did you have to kiss someone like her?*

RichieB01: *Like her? What do you mean?*

Me: *You know – cute, blonde . . . with a small nose?*

RichieB01: *LMAO!!!!!!!! Is that why you're upset? Jesus, Sky, you need some serious help.*

Me: *No I don't. You said you didn't care about my nose, but you did, didn't you? Be honest.*

There's a long pause and I wonder if he's gone offline.

RichieB01: *I can't talk to you when you're like this. Goodbye, Sky. See you around.*

And that is the end of it. He vanishes from the screen, leaving nothing but a greyed-out version of his name.

That's it, then, I think. No more me and Rich. Deep in my heart I probably did know it was over on our anniversary night, but I guess I was too scared to think about it.

I cry again, until my head aches, and then, when I've

calmed down a little, I go on to my Facebook profile and change my status to single. I know I shouldn't check but I can't stop myself. Rich has already deleted me from his friends list. He's probably scared that I might write nasty messages on his wall. Or, maybe somebody else has put up pictures from the party and tagged him and Donna. I feel sick. I'll have to face him at school tomorrow and despite what he's said about being friends he'll probably blank me, which will be horrible. Thank God Donna doesn't go to my school, so I won't have to see them together.

I know I'm not going to get Rich back. But I also know that if I'm ever going to find a boyfriend who loves me, I need to get rid of my nose. I can't wait a minute longer.

Chapter 18

I've Got The Blues

I don't think I've ever felt so down. Every morning, when I wake up, I feel OK for about three short seconds, until I remember again that Rich has dumped me and that I'm going to have to face him across the classroom at school. He's blanking me, just as I predicted he would, acting like he can't see me when I pass him in the corridor, treating me like a stranger – and, worse, one with some horrible, infectious disease – pretending the six months we shared never happened. Yesterday, I'm sure I caught him laughing about me with his mates, drawing pictures of girls with big noses and passing them around. I pretended I hadn't noticed, then went to the toilets to cry. But crying only makes me feel worse – it makes my eyes look small and puffy and my nose bigger and shinier and redder. I am ugly. I am hideous.

Mum is worried about me, because I'm crying all the time and hardly eating anything, but not worried enough to let me have a day off school. She says I need to be brave and strong and stop caring what other people think. She also says that now Rich has revealed his true colours, I should be thankful I'm not with him any more. According to her, I deserve better. But she would say that. She never liked him.

I'm finding it hard to talk to her, or to Ocean or Grass, even to be around them, especially when they're being sweet to me. Grass made me cupcakes the other day, to try to cheer me up and make me eat something, but that just made me cry more. It feels like my big secret – meeting Dad – is wedging itself between us, pushing me apart from them. I want to tell Mum I've found him and talked to him, I really do, and once or twice the words have been on the tip of my tongue, but I know she'll be hurt and angry and that she won't understand. And so every time she hugs me, I feel guilty and two-faced, and push her away.

I've been thinking about Dad a lot. I tried to call him yesterday, just for a chat, but he didn't pick up his phone. He can't have known it was me, he doesn't have my number. The call went to voicemail, one of those generic prerecorded messages that could belong to anyone. I didn't leave a message. I didn't know what to say. A tiny part of me even wondered if he'd given me the right number, or just made one up. He wouldn't have done that, would he? I guess I'll just have to wait until I see him at his next gig.

I do know what would make me feel heaps better about everything: a new nose. At lunchtime today, I rang the clinic and asked if I could schedule my operation, but they wanted a payment up front. I've been saving my allowance (not buying drinks and muffins after school helps) but at this rate it's going to take me until I'm a hundred and fifty before I've saved enough. I've tried getting a part-time job – I asked at Dot's Music Shop – with no luck. Nobody wants to employ a fourteen year old. It's so unfair: I'm not even old enough to buy a lottery ticket. My only option is a loan. From someone, somewhere. Maybe Dad will know where I can get one.

And if that doesn't work? Rob a bank? Sit outside the NatWest on Camden High Street with the homeless people and beg? Change my religion so I have to wear a burkha, which covers my whole face? Maybe I should just cut my nose off myself. Then they'd have to give me an operation to repair it. Who am I kidding? I tried waxing my legs once, with some strips from Boots, and it hurt so much I had to stop in the middle.

No, there's only one thing for it: I think I'll just stay in my room for the rest of my life, with the blind firmly down.

Chapter 19

The Intervention

It's Sunday afternoon. It's been a week now, but I'm not feeling any better. If anything, I feel worse. I hate my life. I hate my nose. I hate my dad for not caring more. I hate Rich too, except I love him. And I hate myself for that. I can't face doing anything: I haven't washed my hair; I'm wearing my pyjamas; I can't even be bothered to put make-up on to disguise my nose, which makes me hate it even more. I hate EVERYONE and EVERYTHING. Especially MYSELF. I wrote that on a piece of paper earlier and it made me feel better for a minute or two, until I hated those stupid words and my horrible, slanted handwriting, and tore the paper into little pieces.

I'm lazing around on my bed now, wondering whether I should climb back in and have a doze, when the doorbell rings. I ignore it. I don't want to see anybody, not even my friends. That's why I haven't been out since I came home from school on Friday and why I've been ignoring their texts. I've even logged out of instant messaging and signed off Facebook. They'll only go on at me about how Rich was a waste of space and how I'm better off without him, and how I'll start to feel happier soon because 'time heals all wounds', and all the other clichés. I don't want to hear it. Why shouldn't I be allowed to feel sorry for myself if I want to?

The doorbell rings again. Longer, this time. It's probably Jehovah's Witnesses. There seem to be an awful lot of them in Camden, and they're very persistent. They must think it's an area where people need extra saving.

'Go away,' I say under my breath. 'Leave me alone.' But the doorbell doesn't listen. I tut. I can hear the hum of the vacuum cleaner from the living room. 'Mum, will you get the door,' I mutter, aware that she won't hear me. I can't even be bothered to raise my voice. Communicating is too much effort.

Mum must have stopped vacuuming because I hear muffled voices and then the buzz of the intercom.

'Sky, will you get out here!' she shouts. She sounds annoyed. 'It's for you. It's *your* friends.' The vacuuming begins again.

I ignore her. I'm going to ignore them too. If they come into my room I'm going to pretend they don't exist. Because I don't exist.

My bedroom door bursts open. No knock. How rude. I turn over and face the wall.

Rosie clambers onto my bed beside me. 'Get up, Sky!'

I ignore her, which is hard, as she's bellowing in my ear.

'Come on, this is getting silly now. We're worried about you.'

I shrug. *Did someone say something?*

'We're not going anywhere, Sky,' says Vix. I can sense that she's standing at the end of the bed. 'So you might as well give up now.'

I ignore her too.

'Do you think she's alive?' asks Rosie. 'She's very quiet. And still. For Sky.'

'Hard to say,' says Vix. 'I think she's sulking. Still, there's only one way to find out.'

I hear them giggle, conspiratorially. Then Rosie counts softly, 'One, two, three,' and suddenly there are hands upon me, all over me, digging into my ribs, under my arms, poking my belly and the underside of my chin, even brushing the soles of my feet. I squirm and twist but I can't escape the tickling hands. They're everywhere, all at once. They're torturing me! I'm trying not to squeal but it's unbearable . . . I can't keep it in any more . . . 'Noooooooo! Aieeee! Hooooo! Heeeeee!' Now I'm laughing, in spite of myself, breathing so hard that I'm becoming light-headed. 'Arghhh! Eeeee! Ohhhh!' I think I'm going to die if they tickle me any more. Has anybody ever died from being tickled? 'Owwww! Ergggg! Oooo!'

They've stopped. Oh, the relief. I lie still, catching my

breath, waiting for my pulse to slow down. Weirdly, I feel better than I have in days, calmer and more relaxed, although I'm not ready to let anyone else know that. I turn my face to the wall again.

'I think she's definitely alive,' says Rosie. 'She made a noise. It didn't sound like a decomposing body to me. She wriggled a lot. And she feels warm too.'

Vix giggles. 'It was a weird noise, though. It sounded more like a creature than a girl. A cat? What do you think, Rosie?'

'Hmm, maybe we should check to make sure.'

I sense their hands coming closer again. Please, no! I leap up, pushing them away from me. It's a reflex action – I'm still trying to pretend they're not there. I won't make eye contact with either of them.

Rosie sighs. 'So, are you going to talk to us now? Because if you don't we're going to tickle you until you speak to us, or really do die. Your choice.'

'Hrmph.' It's all I can manage. I can't endure any more tickling, but speaking actual words would be giving in. 'Pum.'

'That's a start,' says Vix. 'At last.' She sits down beside me on my bed. 'OK, this is what's going to happen. We're going to get you some clothes. You're going to put them on. No arguments.'

I pout. Rosie has already walked over to my wardrobe and is now rifling through my clothes. She returns with my favourite pair of skinny jeans and a newish, sparkly blue top I was saving for a night out. Arguing is futile. I put on the clothes without saying a word. The jeans feel looser than last time I wore them; I guess I must have lost some weight. I haven't even felt like eating chocolate. I sit down on the bed again. Being dressed properly makes me feel better too, although again I don't admit it.

Vix has my hairbrush in her hand. 'You've got such gorgeous hair, Sky,' she says, 'even if it could do with a serious wash. Lucky we brought supplies. Rosie?'

Rosie hands her a bottle of dry shampoo, which she shakes over my scalp. It makes me cough. Then Vix brushes my hair, gently. The sensation is comforting and reminds me of being a little kid. Mum used to do it every night, a hundred strokes. 'Right, now we're going to do your make-up.'

They don't bring me a mirror until they've finished. They've done a good job, although the result is a little more natural than I'd choose. I look healthier, less puffy-eyed, more like me. But they haven't shaded my nose, or put enough powder on it. It shines out at me, beacon-like. Instinctively, I move my hand to cover it.

Vix notices. 'You don't need all that crappy dark stuff on your nose, Sky. You look beautiful without it. Trust me. Trust us.'

I nod, resigned.

Vix takes her phone out of her handbag. 'I'm just going to take a quick snap, OK?'

I nod again, and make an effort at a smile. It's more a grimace. The flash fires.

'OK,' says Rosie. She hands me my bag. 'Have you got your keys?'

I shake my head.

'Get them. We're going out now.'

I must look anxious because she puts her hand on my shoulder, reassuringly. 'Don't worry, not far. Just to my house. OK?'

I really don't want to go out. I REALLY don't want to go out. From somewhere, buried deep inside me, I find my voice. It cracks from lack of use. 'N-o. P-lease. I don't want to.'

'Hey!' Rosie laughs. 'It speaks!'

I pout again.

'Sorry, Sky,' says Vix, 'but you don't have a choice.' She takes one of my arms and Rosie takes the other. They drag me up from the bed and lead me to my door.

'I'll be really bad company,' I protest, pulling back. 'I appreciate you coming round and showing that you care, and I promise I'll text you later and we can meet up soon, but I don't feel like going out now. Just let me be alone.'

'We're not listening,' says Vix, 'and there's no point shouting for your mum. She's in on it too.'

Rosie lets go of me for a second to open my bedroom door. I try to wriggle away. 'You got her?' she asks Vix, who nods. 'Right, let's go.'

I really don't like this. I even feel a little bit scared, although Rosie and Vix are my best friends and I know they'd never do anything to hurt me. 'What are you doing? What's going to happen?'

'Don't be alarmed,' says Rosie, 'but we're staging an

intervention!' It sounds like she's copying a line in a film. If I weren't so miserable and my arms weren't being tugged out of their sockets I might even laugh.

'A what?'

'An intervention. It's what they do to get celebrities to go to rehab when they don't want to.'

'But I'm not a celebrity. And I don't need rehab.'

'Yeah, that's what they all say,' says Rosie, dismissively. 'If anybody needs this, you do. So stop arguing. Either you come with us voluntarily, or we'll have to kidnap you.'

'Or torture you again.' Vix raises her eyebrow provocatively.

No! Anything but the tickling . . . 'OK, OK, I give in.'

'Trust us,' says Vix. 'We only want to help.'

'I don't need help,' I mutter, under my breath. Vix and Rosie exchange 'she's deluded' glances. They think I can't see, but I can, and it niggles me.

I let them lead me down the stairs and out of the front door. We walk up the street, arm in arm, silently. I look straight ahead, feeling sulky and irritated. Halfway along, I contemplate making a run for it, and then think better of that idea. Whatever it is they have planned, I might as well get it over with.

'Here we are,' says Rosie, as we reach her house. Anyone would think I'd never been here before. She loosens her grip so she can fiddle with the keys and open the front door. Once we're inside, she and Vix take me straight upstairs. They pause on the landing, outside Rosie's bedroom door. 'Right, Sky.

Close your eyes and walk slowly into my bedroom. I'll tell you when you can open them.'

'O . . . K . . .'

'No peeking.'

'I said OK!'

Vix takes my hand and leads me into the room. I hear the door being shut gently behind me.

'You can open your eyes now,' says Rosie.

I'm not sure I want to. I open one eye, then the other and blink hard. The room comes into focus. Laid out before me on Rosie's bedroom floor are dozens of printed A4 sheets, all lined up from one wall to the other. As I walk closer I can see that the sheets have images on them, then that they are all portrait photographs of a girl with dark hair. I bend down to pick one up. 'Who's that?' I ask.

Rosie snorts. 'It's you, silly!'

'No it isn't.' I study the picture. It's me, but not me. My face, but not my face. I really don't recognise myself. The girl doesn't look like my dad or my mum or anybody else I know. If this girl turned up at a family reunion, they wouldn't let her in. She looks weird, bland, like a doll or an identifit photo. 'I don't understand.'

'This is you after your nose job,' says Vix. 'We sent your pics to a virtual plastic surgery website. It shows you what you'd look like if your features were changed.'

'It's the same software that the FBI uses,' Rosie interrupts. 'Like in *CSI*. Like when they're trying to find kids who've gone missing years ago, or criminals who've had plastic surgery to evade justice. We just had to send in a pic of you and tell them what you wanted done, and then they doctored your photo so you could see what you'd look like after the operation.' She smiles at me. 'So what do you think of your new nose?'

'I . . . I'm not sure.' I concentrate on the picture again. My new nose is straighter, smaller, more refined, but it seems to throw all my other features off balance. It changes my whole face. My cheeks look fatter, my eyes less expressive, my mouth too big somehow. My face no longer has any character.

'You look weird, don't you?' Rosie says. She bends down and picks up some more pictures, handing each one to me in turn. 'We did tons of variations – gave you lots of different noses.'

'I don't like any of them,' I admit, 'but maybe it's because they're just pictures. Real surgery would be different.'

'No it wouldn't,' says Vix. 'Surgeons use this program. It's realistic. Sky, can't you see that you're really pretty without anything changed? Much prettier, in fact.'

She shows me the photo she took on her phone earlier, then hands me another sheet, with a photo on it that I do recognise. It must be the original picture that they sent in to the website. I don't look pretty in it, but at least I look like me again. And, though I can't say it out loud, I do prefer my face the way it's meant to be. Maybe it isn't possible for me to get rid of my nose and still look like 'me'. That's not something I'd considered before.

Vix is waiting for me to say something. When I don't, she picks up some more sheets and giggles to herself. 'Sorry, but we wanted to have a bit of fun too. Look: this is you with new nose and new eyebrows. We got you Botoxed!'

I stare at it, open mouthed. 'Oh God, I look like Mr Spock out of *Star Trek*.'

'Ha! You're actually making that expression right now.' Vix laughs.

'Want to see what you'd look like with cheek implants and a chin implant?' asks Rosie. 'Oh, and with Angelina Jolie's lips?' She hands over a bundle of sheets.

'Oh my God! I look like the elephant woman! Frankenstein's monster! It's hideous.'

'Yeah,' says Rosie. 'Oh, and we had you aged as well. Want to know what you'll look like at seventy?'

'I'm not sure that I do . . .'

Rosie ignores me. 'Here you go.' She hands me another picture and, there, in front of me, is an old crone, with wrinkles, eye bags and saggy jowls. I look like my grandma . . . in about twenty years.

'I don't look seventy, I look about a thousand! I thought you guys were supposed to be making me feel better, not worse.'

'Sorry, hon,' says Vix. 'We couldn't resist. They said you won't look quite that bad if you keep out of the sun, and if you don't smoke or drink. Anyway, listen, why don't you take the pictures home with you and have a think about them?'

'What, keep them in a drawer so that I never age?'

'Yeah, something like that.'

'OK . . .' I sigh. 'But you do know that I still hate my nose, right? It's not going to be that easy to make me change my mind.'

'Course not,' says Vix. 'And we know you're still down about Rich and everything. Just think about it, OK?'

I nod. 'I promise. Can I go home now?'

'Not if you're going to get all depressed again,' says Rosie. 'Only if you promise to switch your phone back on, log back into Facebook and agree to meet us for coffee after school tomorrow.'

'Maybe,' I say.

Rosie steps in front of me, to block my escape. She shakes her head.

'OK, OK, I promise.' I place my hand on the door handle, before she can change her mind. 'I do love you guys, you know that?'

Vix smiles. 'Yeah, we do. You don't have to thank us.'

I laugh. 'I wasn't going to.'

I'm halfway down the stairs when I hear Rosie coming after me. I quicken my pace, worried that she's going to try to kidnap me again.

'Hey,' she calls out, 'don't forget your photos . . .'

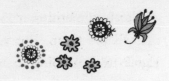

Chapter 20

A Truly Shocking Discovery

The Blues Kitchen is on the corner of Camden High Street and Delancey Street, halfway between Camden Town and Mornington Crescent tube stations. It's bigger and brighter than the Dublin Castle – more a theme venue and restaurant than a pub – with a bourbon bar, pictures of blues stars on the walls and a menu of barbecue ribs and buffalo wings. I haven't brought Vix and Rosie this time, even though Dad invited them. They'd only have got bored again, and I'd have felt bad if I wanted to leave them to talk to Dad alone. Saying that, we probably wouldn't even have got in. When I arrived I had to tell the bouncer I was 'with' the band, and he only let me in because Sarah happened to be coming in at the same time, and vouched for me.

I've told Mum that I've gone round to Rosie's house and that I'll be home by eleven-thirty. Rosie really is seeing Laurie tonight. Vix is staying with a friend and has been warned not to ring me on the home phone. I'm not too happy about the indelible ink stain on the top of my hand, which was stamped on me to prove I'd paid to come in. Somehow, I'll have to scrub it off before Mum notices. I hate having to make all these complicated arrangements, hate telling all these lies, but I don't have a choice, do I? And, compared to the biggest lie of all – the fact that I'm seeing Dad – they're nothing.

The River Runners are on the small stage at the back now, playing almost exactly the same set as last time. I look around me and see many faces that are beginning to become familiar. The dark-haired girl is here again, swaying in time to the music, mouthing the words. She seems to know nearly all the songs off by heart. I wonder how long she's been going out with Dad. She's probably just like the woman he left Mum for: young, good-looking, with no children or responsibilities. I'm sure he'll dump her too, soon enough. I'm going to ask him about her tonight.

I'm feeling much better than I was even just a few days ago, missing Rich less (as I dislike him more), spending time with my friends, feeling like myself. I wouldn't say I've fully got my appetite back, but chocolate tastes good again. Even my nose is featuring less prominently in my thoughts (although, unfortunately, not on my face). Every night, I take the pictures Rosie and Vix gave me out of my bedside drawer and study them. At first I did it to try to get used to my new face, so that I'd be prepared for how I'd look after the operation, but that didn't really work. Rosie and Vix have been keeping up their campaign. They did some more internet research and found several scary web forums about Dr Sierra, with former patients saying he'd butchered them and that they were suing. Rosie made me swear that even if I do decide to have a nose job one day, ('which you DON'T need') I will find someone else to do it. I said that they don't have to worry: until I can afford to pay for surgery, there's nothing I can do about my nose, except live with it. And breathe through it. And blow it, too, occasionally. Vix says the fact I can make jokes about it again is a very good sign.

Dad's coming offstage now. I caught his eye while he was playing and he winked at me, and it made me feel special, like he did care and he was pleased I'd made it. But he isn't coming over to me now; he's going straight to the bar to get a drink and talk to his friends. I haven't managed to chat to him at all since the last gig, even though I've rung a few times. He did pick up once, told me he was rehearsing and that he'd call me back later. He didn't.

I stand on my own by one of the booths, feeling like a mis-shape in a chocolate box, wondering whether I should go over to him. Eventually, Shane spots me and beckons me over to join the group.

'Hello again, Sky, can I get you a drink?'

'Yes, please,' I say, gratefully. 'Just a lime and soda.' I think it sounds more sophisticated than a Diet Coke.

'Coming right up. So did you enjoy the gig?'

'Yes, it was good.'

He laughs. 'I guess it's not really your type of music. You don't have any blues on your MP-wotsit player?'

I'm embarrassed. 'No, but I kind of like it. I remember some of the tunes from Dad's CDs when I was little.'

'There's hope for your generation yet, then. Hear that, Connor, your daughter likes a bit of blues.'

Dad turns around and puts his arm across my shoulder. 'Course she does.'

I sip my drink and join in with the banter for a while, wondering how I will ever get Dad on his own for a proper conversation. When he announces that he's going outside for a cigarette, I seize my opportunity. 'Can I come out with you, Dad?'

'Sure,' he says. 'Do you want one?'

'No! I'm only fourteen, remember. I don't smoke. I just want to talk to you.'

'Ah, aye. OK.'

I follow him outside and we stand with all the other smokers, puffing away. I wonder how I'm going to explain to Mum why my clothes stink of smoke. I'll have to tell her that Rosie has started smoking.

'So what did you want to talk to me about?'

'You know, just stuff.'

'Stuff?' He seems uncomfortable. In fact, the expression on his face is just like the one Rich used to make when I told him I wanted to talk. Are all guys like that? Or am I just unlucky?

'About you, me, life . . . You haven't really told me anything about what you've been up to since you left.'

'Not much to tell, really. I've been touring, living here and there, all over the country. Had a few girlfriends. Nothing special. I'm a "wherever I lay my hat" type of guy. Easy come, easy go.'

He doesn't mention being homeless. Or the fact he lived in Camden for a while.

'Why didn't you stay in touch with us?'

'I did at first. But your mother didn't want anything to do with me. It made it hard. And I didn't have any money to send. I figured you were all doing fine without me.'

'Oh. But we missed you. *I* missed you.'

'I thought about you girls all the time, always had your photos with me. I knew we'd see each other again, one day.'

He gives me a brief hug, then pinches my cheek, as if that's supposed to make everything all right. 'Come on,' he says, dropping the end of his cigarette and stamping on the butt. 'Let's go back inside and sit down in one of the booths.'

He waits until I'm seated, then goes to the bar again, returning with two more drinks. 'Let's talk about you instead. Much more interesting. Do you have a boyfriend?'

I sigh. 'Bad subject. I did have, but it's finished. I don't really want to talk about it.'

'Aye, I know what it's like. You're a pretty girl, I'm sure there will be lots of lads all queuing up to date you.'

I roll my eyes. 'Seriously? Where? Anyway, tell me about your girlfriend. Have you been together long?'

'Girlfriend? Which girlfriend?'

'The one over there at the bar, talking to some of your fans. The one who was at your last gig too. She looks dead young, long dark hair.'

'Long dark hair?' He nods in her direction. 'Oh, you mean Katie!' He laughs heartily, as though this is the funniest thing he's ever heard. 'She wouldn't be interested in an old fellow like me. Katie's not my girlfriend. She's my daughter.'

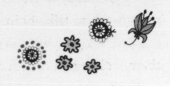

Chapter 21

My Sister Katie

'Your daughter? But that means she's my *sister*!' I'm numb with shock. So numb that I don't even laugh nervously.

'Aye. Well, more accurately, your half-sister. Can't you see the resemblance? You're two peas in a pod, so you are.'

Something Reg said at Dot's Music Shop now comes back to me. '*He had some photos that he put above his bed. All pretty girls, his daughters. A couple of you just like him too.*' I remember, at the time, thinking that it was a strange thing to say – Ocean and Grass look nothing like my dad. Reg must have been talking about Katie all along. He must have seen a photo of her.

'I don't understand, Dad.' Nothing makes any sense. Katie must be older than Ocean, at least nineteen or twenty. How can that be? 'How old is she, Dad?'

'Ah, you know I'm not good at ages. She's around twenty, twenty-one I think.' He furrows his brow. 'Yes, twenty-one.'

'But that means . . .' That means Dad had a family before he met Mum. That means that for the whole of my life, I've had a sister I didn't know about. A living, breathing sister who's been calling my dad *Dad*, going to his gigs, maybe even living with him.

I look over at her, watch as she talks to some guy at the bar and throws her head back in laughter, oblivious, and I realise that I feel horribly jealous of this girl who shares my dad's affections. How much time did he spend with her when I was little? How much money did he give her, when we had to go without because he was broke? All those times he went away 'on tour' – was he really with her, with his other family?

'I don't understand,' I say again. 'How? Who's her mum?'

'A girl I knew way back, before I met your mother. We weren't together long.'

'So Katie's never lived with you?'

'Oh no. It wasn't like that. Her mother and I split up before she was born.'

'So how come she's here now?'

'Same reason you are,' he says. 'She tracked me down. A few years ago. She comes along to some of my gigs.'

'God, Dad! Do you have any other kids I should know

about?' I blush. I didn't mean to say that out loud. But I need to know; I can't handle any more secrets, any more surprises.

Dad grins, perhaps a little too mischievously. 'Not that I know of, no.'

'Right. Good. But what about my mum? Does she know about Katie?'

'Aye, she does. Katie was a baby when we got together. She met her once or twice.'

Now I'm angry with Mum. My mind is whirring. Why didn't she tell us? I have a right to know that I have a half-sister, don't I? Maybe I'd have liked the opportunity to get to know her. We could have been friends, closer than I am to Ocean and Grass. What if she'd been a boy, not a girl, and we'd bumped into each other and fallen in love . . .? It's all just too weird to think about. 'Does Katie know about us, about your other family? Does she know who I am?'

I remember thinking that the girl – Katie – might have been smiling at me earlier, when she caught me staring at her. I didn't smile back. I just looked away. But that was when I thought she was Dad's girlfriend.

Dad appears uncomfortable. 'She knows I have other daughters. She knows your name. She was asking about you, wondering who you were. I said I didn't think you knew about her. Maybe I should introduce the two of you.'

My stomach flips over. I'm not sure if I'm ready for that. Five minutes ago, I wasn't aware that Katie existed. 'Um, I don't know . . . Maybe, yes, you should, I guess.'

'All right. Stay there,' he says, before I can change my mind. He picks up his pint from the table and walks over to the bar, leaving me sitting alone, unsure what to do with myself. I fiddle with my hair and cross and uncross my legs, trying to pretend that everything is normal. I watch as he walks up to her and whispers something in her ear. She smiles, swings her handbag over her shoulder, and the two of them start heading towards me. Dad catches my eye and winks.

They're here. Oh God. How do you greet the sister you didn't know you had? I take a deep breath, trying to calm my nerves, certain that my voice, if I still have one, will come out in a high-pitched squeak.

'Hi,' she says. 'I'm Katie.'

I try to scramble up to meet her but my seat is too close to the table. I sit down again, clumsily. 'I'm Sky.'

She leans over to kiss me on the cheek and, at the same time, I hold out my hand. We both giggle, awkwardly.

'OK, I'll leave you girls to it,' says Dad. He seems relieved. He wanders back over to the bar, leaving me alone with Katie. We sit in silence for a moment, grinning at each other.

'Um, nice to meet you,' I say. 'Um, this is weird.'

Katie laughs. 'Yeah. On a scale of weirdness, this is about a hundred. Must be weirder for you, though. Dad says you didn't even know about me till tonight.'

I bristle when she calls him Dad. Now that's *really* weird. But she seems all right – warm, friendly. I feel comfortable with her, even in this bizarre situation. Instantly comfortable, like I can talk to her about anything.

'I'm sorry if I was rude, earlier. I thought you were Dad's girlfriend. It made me sort of hate you. I don't even know why.'

'Oh good God, you didn't, did you? Ha! Believe me, he's really not my type. Even if he weren't my dad. Eugh! Funny, I thought you were just acting cool. A cool Camdenite. I meet a lot of them when I work around here.'

'Me, cool? No way!'

'You look pretty cool,' she says. 'I love your hair, and your style.'

'Really? Thanks. I like what you're wearing too. So what do you do? In your work, I mean?'

'Well, mainly I'm a student – art – at the Slade. It's part of UCL, up the road. That's how come I ended up living round here. But I also work as a DJ, doing parties and clubs. My moniker is Lady Luscious. I didn't come up with it!'

'Wow, now that's *really* cool.'

She grins. 'Thanks. I love DJing, and the money's not bad. Most of all, I love the music.'

'Yeah? Do you like R&B? I saw Bizzie Trip in Camden recently. At the MTV studios. I totally heart him.'

'He's OK,' she says. 'Not bad. I prefer slightly more alternative stuff. I'll play you some of my tracks if you like, some time.'

'Yeah, I'd love that. I wish I knew how to DJ.'

'I can teach you.'

'Seriously?'

'Yeah. Why not? It might be fun. I've always wanted a little sister.'

'When all along you had three of us.'

'Yeah.' She chews her lip. 'I don't know if I should say this but I actually used to hate you too – not you personally – but all of you, the idea of you. I thought you'd stolen my dad. You were all playing happy families with him, while me and Mum had to cope on our own.'

'It wasn't like that . . . He only stuck around till I was eight, and before that he wasn't around much either, always away on tour. He used to drink a lot. We never had any money.'

She smiles. 'I know. Don't worry, I didn't make voodoo dolls of you and stick pins in them, or anything like that. Although I was tempted.'

'Phew! So how did you find Dad?'

'My mum is a musician too – she teaches violin – and she knew a few people on the circuit who knew what he was up to. When I came to uni, I did a bit of Googling, found a gig he was playing at and pitched up.'

'Wow, that's almost the same as me.' I don't say "except for the mum part". 'So have you seen a lot of him since? Got to know him?'

She stares at me, dead in the eyes. 'I don't want to make you sad, but no, not really. He doesn't seem to want to play Dad. We've met up a couple of times – and *not* met a few more times when he didn't show. He's pretty unreliable. Mostly I just see him when he's in town, playing gigs. He seems happy with that, to have me around, but at a distance. I don't even know much about his life, where he lives. I've never been invited round.'

'Oh.' I feel suddenly tearful, even though I'm not that surprised. I was hoping that Mum was wrong about Dad, that he'd changed. It sounds like he never will.

She puts her hand on my shoulder. 'Sorry, Sky. I didn't mean to upset you. Maybe he'll be different with you. But I don't think so. And it's better that you don't get your hopes up. He's good company, fun to be around and I think he does love us. Just not the way he should, maybe.'

'OK.'

She grins. 'Hey, Dad thinks we look alike. We do, actually.'

'Do you think so, honestly?' I study her face. I wish I did look like her. She's gorgeous, effortlessly so. 'You're much prettier than me. I have this hideous nose. Everyone says it's Dad's nose.' I cradle it in my palm, wondering why I'm stupid enough to have drawn attention to it.

'What? This nose?' She points to her own nose, turning to the side so that I can see her profile. 'Mine's almost exactly the same. Look.'

'No, I didn't even notice your nose. Mine is much bigger.'

'Rubbish.'

'You're just being kind, like everyone else is. I've been trying to get a nose job. But I don't have the money. And most people say I'm too young . . . that it's still going to grow!'

She shakes her head and frowns. 'No way! You don't want a nose job! Think of all the snot and the blood, and the black eyes. I didn't like mine either, when I was younger. It's kind of grown on me.' She giggles. 'If you know what I mean. Not bigger, just better.'

'Yeah, everyone says that too. *You'll get used to it, Sky. It gives you character. Blah, blah, blah.* My best friends even got pictures of what I'd look like after surgery to help talk me out of it. It's helped, a bit, I guess. I'm not quite as paranoid as I used to be . . . Maybe if it was a teeny bit smaller, like yours, I'd be OK with it.'

She sighs. 'Oh Sky. Right. Follow me.' She gets out of her chair and takes my hand, so that I have to get up too. 'I'll prove it to you.'

'Where are you taking me?'

'You'll see.'

She leads me across the pub to the Ladies, taking me straight to the sinks. The lighting is dreadful, and the mirror cracked and dirty. She pulls a tissue out of her handbag and wipes it.

'Right,' she says, turning to the side and pushing her face against it. 'Take my lipstick and draw around the outline of my nose.'

'What? Are you serious?'

'Yes, go on.'

I giggle. 'OK. You're bonkers!' I do as she says, recreating her profile in bright red lipstick on the mirror. It's hard to get close enough without painting her actual nose. When I've finished, she has three bright red spots on the bridge.

'Cool. My turn now.' She gives the mirror another wipe, a few centimetres away from my drawing. 'Hold your face still.'

At that moment a woman comes out of one of the cubicles and gives us a funny look. We both collapse into giggles. She washes her hands, and dries them, pretending not to notice us.

'Hold still, Sky. Otherwise you'll have a squiggly nose.'

I let Katie draw around my profile – something I probably wouldn't have let anyone do just a few weeks ago. It tickles. As she finishes, she paints a red spot on my nostril.

'There you go – you've got a nose stud.'

'I used to have one of those,' I tell her. 'Took it out.'

'I bet it would suit you.'

'Hmm.'

'OK, stand back,' says Katie. 'Look at what we've drawn.'

I take a step backwards. This is probably the craziest, weirdest situation ever. Half an hour ago, I didn't even know I had a sister. Now, here we are, comparing lipstick noses in a toilet mirror. I can't wait to tell Vix and Rosie about this.

'Tell me what you see.'

'Um . . .' I have to admit it: our nose outlines are virtually identical, the same shape and size, with the same bump. Mirror images, on the mirror.

'We have the same nose! Don't we?' says Katie.

'I guess.'

'Not bigger, not smaller, not straighter. Exactly the same.'

'Yeah, but maybe my face is smaller.'

'Bollocks,' she says, grabbing my cheek. 'If you don't admit I'm right I'm going to paint red lipstick all over your face, got it?'

'OK, OK!'

'Good. Honestly Sky, believe me. You look great. And if you're ugly, then so am I. Do you think I'm ugly?'

'No, course not.'

'Good. OK, let's go back to the table.'

She takes my hand again, and starts leading me to the door.

'What about our noses on the mirror? Aren't you going to wipe them off?'

She turns and glances at our handiwork. 'Nah, they can stay. Look at the state of the mirror, already. Call it a new type of graffiti – it'll get people wondering. Better wipe our noses though. We look like we've had a punch-up.' She hands me a tissue.

Back at our table, we talk about boys, studying, our lives. I tell her about Rich, and she tells me about a relationship with a guy she really loved, which recently ended. Talking to her is so much easier than talking to my full sisters, even though I've known them all my life. It feels like she's one of my closest friends, already.

We're both aware it's late now. She picks my phone up from the table and enters her details straight into my address book. 'Text me yours,' she says. 'And give me a call and we'll arrange for you to come round.'

'I'd love to. Thanks. Are you sure?'

'Yes, I'm not like our dad. I mean it. I'd really like to spend some time getting to know you better. Like I said, I've always wanted a sister. There was only me and Mum. Hey, maybe you could bring your other sisters too.'

'Oh,' I say, and my expression must give my thoughts away.

'Oh dear. They don't know you're here, do they?'

I look down, sheepish. 'No. I haven't told anyone in my family that I've met Dad. Only my best friends, Vix and Rosie know. My sisters, Ocean and Grass – I know, we've all got bad names – aren't exactly Dad's biggest fans. My mum doesn't even like talking about him.'

'Hmm. Well, maybe you could bring your friends instead some time.'

'Cool. I'm sure they'd love to meet you.'

'But Sky, you really should talk to your mum about this. You need to tell her you've met your dad – and me. Really. It's not good to have such a big secret. It will eat away at you.'

I nod. 'I know.'

'If you want to talk about it, or just need a friendly ear, you can call me, anytime. OK?'

'OK. Thank you.'

'No problem.' She gets up from the table. 'Right, I'd better get you back or your mum will be sending out a search party. Get your coat and say goodbye to Dad. I'll walk you home.'

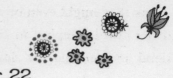

Chapter 22

Coming Clean

osie and Vix couldn't believe it when I told them how I went to the gig to see my dad and came home a few hours later with a sister I didn't know I had. It does sound crazy when you put it like that. And that's not all. When Katie walked me home that night, she seemed surprised and said she recognised my street. It turns out she knows some of the people who live in the art collective – the one that Rosie sneaked into with Rufus Justice once. Katie's even been to a party there and stayed the night. Just think, I was tucked up in bed that night, totally unaware that my own sister was sleeping just a few doors away. It blows my mind.

My friends both said they were really keen to meet Katie

as soon as they can, especially when they found out she DJs. I think they might even be a little jealous. Katie has been true to her word, keeping in touch, making me her Facebook friend and sending me silly texts. I went round to her flat yesterday for lunch and met her flatmates. Her artwork is amazing: huge canvasses with incredible colours and thick paint spattered everywhere. Next week, she's going to give me a DJing lesson on her decks. I can't wait.

But there's something I have to do first. Something horrible and scary, but equally unavoidable. I have to tell Mum the truth. I've been putting it off for too long, scared of what will happen, of how she'll react. Most of all, I don't want to hurt her. But, just as Katie warned, it's beginning to eat away at me, making me feel less and less close to my family, making it impossible for me to be myself around any of them. I'm short with them and snappy, and they think it's because I'm still upset about Rich. It's not: it's because I feel guilty. So, whatever happens, even if Mum never speaks to me again, or throws me out on the street, or confiscates my iPod, at least I'll have got it off my chest.

I've asked if I can speak to her alone tonight, after dinner. We're in her bedroom, sitting on her bed. I've always liked this room, with its bright green Indian throw and gold scatter cushions, and incense burning on the dresser. I feel comfortable in here, calm, relaxed.

'I've been so worried about you lately, Sky,' Mum says. 'I'm so pleased you've finally decided to talk to me.'

Her sweetness makes me feel even more guilty about what I'm planning to tell her. I look down at my hands, weave my fingers in and out of each other. 'I don't know how to say this. I don't know where to begin.'

'What is it, love? Whatever it is, I'm sure I can help.'

'It isn't . . . You won't . . . I did something that I know you didn't want me to do . . . I found Dad.'

She flinches, as if someone has slapped her. 'How? When?'

'Through the internet. A few weeks ago.'

She can't look at me. 'When you say *found*, do you mean tracked down, or *actually met*?'

'Um . . .' I suppose I need to tell her everything now. No point leaving out any details to soften it – apart from the bit about Reg, which will only worry her. 'Both.'

'Right,' she says. 'Right. When?'

'About a month ago.'

'I see. And how did you find him?'

'With a bit of detective work, on the internet, mainly.'

In spite of herself, she seems amused. 'No, I meant, how did he seem to you? Is he well?'

'Um . . .' I'm torn between not wanting to hurt Mum and not wanting to be disloyal to Dad. 'He's OK. Actually, he looks old and grey and fat, like he doesn't look after himself properly, if that makes you feel any better.'

'I don't wish him any ill, whatever you think. So what has he been doing?'

'This and that,' I say, echoing his own words. I'm

embarrassed to admit that I've learned so little. 'Drifting around, I think.'

'I see. And have you seen him just the once? Or have you kept in touch?'

'Sort of. I've seen him a couple of times, at gigs. But he doesn't really seem to want to spend much time with me.' It's hard to admit that she was right, hard to admit to myself that Dad isn't that interested in getting to know me again. It hurts.

Mum moves up closer to me and gives me a hug. She strokes my hair and, hard as it must be for her, smiles at me, a brave little smile. I was expecting her to be angrier – it might be easier if she were – but she just seems sad. And it strikes me now that, if I strip away my excitement at the adventures I've had, underneath I feel sad too.

I pull away. 'I'm sorry,' I say. 'Not sorry I found Dad, but sorry if I've upset you.'

'You don't have to be sorry. I think I knew you would, eventually. I was hoping you would wait until you were older. I was only trying to protect you. I didn't want you to get hurt. I guess you're growing up faster than I'd like.'

I can't stop now. 'There's something else.' I try to meet her eyes, but she's staring across the room, focusing on the paintwork. 'I've met my sister Katie too.'

'Oh?' She sounds far more surprised about this than about Dad. Or maybe it's her turn to feel guilty; she knows she's never told me about Katie.

'She was at Dad's gig. He introduced me to her. She only

lives up the road, in Holloway. She's a student here. Coincidence, huh?'

'Yes, I suppose it is.'

'Katie's really nice. We get on really well. You'd like her, honest.'

'I'm sure she is. No reason why she shouldn't be. I have no truck with her.'

'Why didn't you ever mention her, then?'

'I'm sorry. Maybe I should have. But there didn't seem any point, not when your dad wasn't in contact with any of us. I haven't heard about her since she was a baby.'

'That makes sense, I guess.' I hesitate, not sure how to end my confession. 'So, Mum, that's all of it. Are you going to punish me? Ground me? Because you can't stop me seeing Dad or Katie. I'll run away if you do.'

She shakes her head. 'Punish you? Now what would be the point of that? Of course I'm not happy with the way you've gone about things, but I understand why you needed to do it. And I can't deny you a relationship with your father, or your half-sister, if you want one. But no more sneaking around or lying. No more going behind my back. No more secrets. From now on, you have to be honest with me.'

'Really?' I'm going to get off scot-free? She's not even going to try to stop me meeting them? 'I promise, Mum.' Now it's my turn to hug her. Despite her hippy–dippy ways and her horrible vegetarian concoctions and her weird taste in music, she really is all right, my mum. I'm lucky, I guess.

'Just understand this, Sky,' she says, her voice muffled by my hair. 'I do not want to see your dad. He's not to come round here. OK?'

I can't imagine a situation when that could ever happen. 'Yes, of course. What about Ocean and Grass? Should I tell them?'

'I don't know. Let's think about it. Play it by ear. Deal?'

'Deal.'

'Thanks, Mum,' I say, as I climb off her bed. 'I wish I'd told you weeks ago.'

Chapter 23

Lady Luscious

'*Everybody put your hands in the air!*'

Rosie takes one of my arms, and Vix the other, and we wave them about in time to the music, laughing at each other, having a fantastic time. It's Saturday night and we're on the dancefloor at the Electric Ballroom, just by Camden Town tube – an indoor market during the day, and a music venue at night. I'm wearing my newish sparkly blue top, a short black skirt and my highest platforms, and everyone has told me I look really good. For once, I haven't contradicted them. I've even put my nose stud back in for the night. Just to see how I like it.

We're here for an under-eighteens club night and Lady

Luscious (aka my sister Katie) is DJing. Practically everybody I know is in the room: my friends, Ocean, people from school, even Rich. He just looked over and smiled at me. I pretended I hadn't noticed. It's cruel, I know, but satisfying. And no worse than the way he's treated me. He only wants anything to do with me again because he's heard I know the DJ, so suddenly I'm worth knowing. That, and (ha ha) things didn't last with Donna.

Now that I've had six weeks to think about it, I can see that our break-up wasn't entirely his fault: I know I must have been a pain to be around when I was absolutely fixating on my nose, but maybe if he'd been just a tiny bit more understanding and sensitive, it would have helped. Mum has this theory that my feelings for Rich were really about filling the gap left by Dad. I told her that sounds very airy fairy, and weird, but between you and me, maybe she's right.

All I know is that I haven't missed him half as much as I thought I would. I realise that it was more the idea of him that I was in love with, the person I wanted him to be, rather than the immature guy he is. I don't need a boyfriend, not one who doesn't make me happy. Anyway, Vix and Rosie are having French exchange students to stay for a month soon. They don't know who they're getting yet, but they've told me that some of them will be boys, and we all know that French boys are hot. Much hotter than Rich. So you never know . . .

I haven't seen Dad since the gig at the Blues Kitchen, but that's OK. He actually picked up the phone when I rang him the other day, and we had a little chat. He's promised that we'll have a coffee some time and he even gave me an address in Clapham (I'm not sure if it's where he lives, or just a friend's) so I could send him a more up-to-date picture of me. I decided to give him the one Vix took of me on the day of the intervention. (I did toy with the idea of sending one of the 'after my operation' pics, just as a joke, but nobody else thought it was funny.) I've been keeping track of The River Runners online, so I know he's playing in Camden again soon, and that I'll definitely see him then.

Not having a real father-daughter relationship, like the one I imagined, would hurt more if it weren't for Katie. We've seen quite a bit of each other the past few weeks, and we're really close now. I've had a couple of DJing lessons and she's said that she might even let me have a go on her decks later tonight – if I'm feeling brave enough and promise not to break them. She's also been helping me with my coursework and teaching me about art. Her favourite artist is this Mexican woman called Frieda Kahlo, who (mainly) painted portraits of herself in the nineteen-twenties and thirties. She was incredibly striking, with mad bushy eyebrows that met in the middle (and a bit of a moustache, but maybe they didn't have bleach in those days). Katie thinks she's beautiful, in her own way, much more beautiful than girls like Donna, and I'm beginning to see what she means.

Mum and I talked things over, again, and decided it was only fair to tell Ocean and Grass about Katie. She came round for tea last weekend. She brought chocolate cake. Everyone likes her, although I think Ocean is finding it difficult to adjust to not being my only big sister any more.

'Everybody in the house, this is a shout out to someone special. Sky – this one's for you!'

Oh my God! Katie has just dedicated a song to me: she's playing the latest Bizzie Trip track. She waves at me from the DJ booth and I wave back, with the biggest grin on my face. I haven't stopped smiling all night. My feet hurt and I'm sweaty, and God knows how shiny my face is, but I don't mind. Honestly. I'm dancing with my two best friends, totally unselfconsciously, not caring what anyone else thinks. Out of the corner of my eye, I catch sight of my nose, the little jewelled stud glinting in rhythm with the club lights. And do you know what? Tonight, at least, I think it's OK. I can live with it.

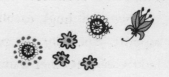

Acknowledgements

Thanks to Brenda Gardner, Anne Clark, Andrea Reece, Melissa Hyder, Natasha Barnden, and everyone at Piccadilly Press for publishing this book.

Many thanks to Stephanie Thwaites and Catherine Saunders at Curtis Brown, and thank you and hello to my new agent, Catherine Pellegrino.

A huge thank you to the real life Dot Fraser of Dot's Music Shop for allowing me to feature a fictionalised version of her in the book.

Thanks to all my Facebook friends for help with band and character names (and for allowing me to vent), notably Matthew McCarthy who came up with the winner,

The River Runners.

Love and hugs to all my family and friends for your support, especially my parents, Steve Somerset, Claire Fry, Judy Corre, Rachel Baird, Jax Donnellan, Diane Messidoro, Janet Smith and Luisa Plaja of *Chicklish*.

Thanks to Laura D at Waterstone's.

Merci to everyone at the Citea Nice Magnan, where much of this book was written (in room 616) – particularly to Marlene, Julie and Mickael. Still working on that French translation for you!

Finally, thanks to the rioters of Camden Town for not destroying any landmarks featured in this series.

And RIP Amy Winehouse.

Camden Town Tales

The Celeb Next Door

Hilary Freeman

Rosie has lived in Paradise Avenue, Camden Town all her life. As well as the market to hang out at and gigs to go to, there are celebrities to spot, and TV studios where she and her best friends Sky and Vix might get noticed.

When Rosie finds out that the drummer from a chart-topping group is moving into the house next door, she makes it her mission to befriend him. But things don't turn out quite the way she expects . . .

Coming Soon
Camden Town Tales

Book 3

Hilary Freeman

Look out for the third fabulous book in the Camden Town Tales series!

Life becomes more Ooh la la when French exchange students come to stay with Vix and Rosie. Will they love Camden as much as the girls? Or will there be more than just cultures clashing?

CamdenTownTales.co.uk

Join us online for:

- 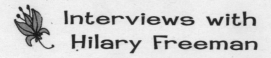 **The Insider's Guide to Camden Town**

- **Interviews with Hilary Freeman**

- **The latest on the Camden Town Tales books**

Find us on Facebook for competitions, exclusive content and more!